The Harem

Safia Fazlul

We acknowledge the support of the Canada Council for the Arts for our publishing program. We also acknowledge support from the Government of Ontario through the Ontario Arts Council.

We acknowledge the financial support of the Government of Canada through the Canada Book Fund for our publishing activities.

ONTARIO ARTS COUNCIL
CONSEIL DES ARTS DE L'ONTARIO

Canada Council Conseil des Arts
for the Arts   du Canada

Canada

Cover art by Safia Fazlul
Cover design by Peggy Stockdale

Library and Archives Canada Cataloguing in Publication

Fazlul, Safia
    The harem / Safia Fazlul.

ISBN 978-1-894770-98-9

    I. Title.

PS8611.A98H37 2012   C813'.6   C2012-905115-2

Printed and bound in Canada by Coach House Printing

TSAR Publications
P. O. Box 6996, Station A
Toronto, Ontario M5W 1X7
Canada

www.tsarbooks.com

To my sister,
Nipa Haque

One day in 1989 . . .

"I don't want to go!"

"You must go."

Every Sunday morning just before leaving for her Islamic class at the Peckville Community centre, little Farina Farooki would beg her mother to let her stay home.

Although Mrs Farooki felt sorry for her pouting daughter, she was adamant about her attending the Islamic class. Knowing the teachings of the Quran was crucial for her daughter's upbringing. With two jobs and a husband who refused to lift a finger to help her in the home, Mrs Farooki had no time to teach what was right and what was wrong to her child. She hoped that God would do the job for her.

Mrs Farooki grabbed Farina by the shoulders and ordered her to stand still. As she began to wrap a scarf around the seven-year-old's head, she said delicately in Bengali, "You will be right back here with me within a few hours. I'm going to make you beef biryani and I'll feed you while we watch TV together, okay?"

A smile formed on Farina's face at the very mention of her mother watching TV with her. It was a rare opportunity. Factories stole Mrs Farooki away from Farina during the day. By night, the physical toll of their demands would have transformed the usually lively woman into a weary bore. Ever since she left Bangladesh for Canada three years ago, she had hardly had the time to watch television with her only child.

Mrs Farooki smiled back at the happy little face. The scarf on Farina's rich black hair did nothing to subtract from her beauty. She told her daughter to face her father and asked him, "Is there any girl cuter than our daughter?"

Mr Farooki didn't look up from the TV but grunted his agreement. He was sitting on the couch with nothing but a sarong wrapped around his thin waist, flipping through the channels and quite oblivious of his wife's furious glare.

Farina watched her mysterious father with curiosity. Although he worked the same long hours as her mother, she knew a lot less about him. He didn't talk much. When he did open his mouth, it was almost always to yell at her mother. Whether it was a tiny spot on the floor or a little dust on the TV, he always had something to scream about. Farina found it strange that her parents arrived home at the same time every weeknight, but only her mother went directly to the kitchen to make dinner. Her father did nothing but complain about all the housework that needed to be done. Maybe it was just normal for women to keep quiet and take orders from their husbands.

A sudden knock on the door distracted Mrs Farooki's attention from her sluggish husband.

"I want to open it! I want to open it!" Farina chanted eagerly while her mother held her fixed.

As Mrs Farooki zipped up Farina's sweater all the way up, she said sharply to her husband, "Ahmed Bhabhi's here, go put on a shirt!"

Mr Farooki glowered at his wife. She was not allowed to give him any orders—especially not on a Sunday, the only day of the week he didn't spend washing dishes at a restaurant. He decided to deal with this affront later only because they had a guest at the door. He turned the TV off and hurried to the bedroom. He locked himself inside as Mrs Farooki muttered some Bengali profanities to herself. Her lazy husband would rather hide than get dressed.

Another knock prompted Farina to escape her mother's grip, skip to the door, and fling it open. Farina jumped with joy at the sight of Imrana and her mother. The two kids pounced into each other's arms and giggled.

"We look so weird," Imrana said to a nodding Farina and they both tugged at the edge of their headscarves.

"Chup!" Imrana's mother hushed her daughter and greeted Mrs Farooki, "As-Salamu Alaykum, Bhabhi."

Farina and Imrana playfully mimicked their chitchatting mothers, who spoke in Bengali, with its typical mannerisms, tilting their heads and moving their hands. To the girls, who were used to speaking in English, Bengali sounded like comical gibberish.

Mrs Farooki saw the girls and lost her patience. "Take these two sinners to class now, Bhabhi. They're not learning how to be good people at their white school."

Mrs Farooki kissed Farina on the forehead before shoving her towards Mrs Ahmed.

"Yes, we'd better go before we're late."

"Thank you so much. When you come back, please stay for some tea. Khuda-Hafeez. God Bless," and Mrs Farooki shut the door.

The walls in Farina's building were so thin that voices readily escaped from the apartments into the halls. While Farina, Imrana, and Mrs Ahmed waited for the elevator they could clearly hear Mr Farooki shouting at his wife in Bengali. He used words that Farina didn't know the meanings of, but they always made her mother cry. Farina squeezed Imrana's hand tightly. Mrs Ahmed pretended not to hear. She praised little Farina for her good marks in school, as if that would help the child ignore her father's shouts.

༺

After fastening Farina and Imrana to their seats, Mrs Ahmed drove her sedan to a neighbouring building. There was one more sinner to pick up for Islamic class.

Mrs Ahmed sighted a small figure inside the foyer of the building. She was glad she didn't have to get out of the car. She disliked the little girl who was waiting. As the girl paced closer to the car,

Farina and Imrana shouted cheerfully together, "Sabrina!"

Sabrina Jahan, Farina's best friend and Imrana's idol, was especially unhappy about having her curly black locks covered. Ducking her head she stepped into the car and didn't react when Farina hugged her tightly.

"Sabrina, where is your mom? It's not good to stand here alone. There are black boys everywhere," Mrs Ahmed reproached her as she leaned over to fix Sabrina's seatbelt.

"Mom is upstairs, Auntie. I know how to come down the elevator on my own," Sabrina said proudly as the other two girls admired her smart response. "She told me to say hi to you, Auntie."

Mrs Ahmed smiled and continued on the road. She turned her CD player on and a popular Bollywood song played quietly in the background. The girls didn't understand the Hindi lyrics of the song, but they enjoyed the music. To Mrs Ahmed's surprise, the trio were completely silent. But the silence ended as soon as the song did.

"I look so ugly!" Sabrina complained to her friends.

"No, you don't." Farina lay her head on Sabrina's shoulder. She loved Sabrina. Nobody could be prettier, not even blonde, blue-eyed Barbie. "You never look ugly."

Imrana stretched out of her seat to look at Sabrina. Her eyes became wide as she said with utter passion, "Sabrina, you are the prettiest girl in the whole world!"

Imrana's mother chuckled at her daughter's exaggeration. "No, Imrana, Farina is also the prettiest girl in the world. You are lucky to have two best friends who are both so fair."

Imrana sank back into her seat, looking dejected. This wasn't the first time that her mother had equated her friends' light skins to their prettiness. Rather dark in complexion, Imrana was sure that her mother found her ugly.

Farina and Sabrina blushed at Mrs Ahmed's compliment. Before they could thank their auntie, they were told to take their seatbelts off. They had arrived at the Community Centre.

Mrs Ahmed watched the girls' colourful knapsacks flapping against their backs as they made their way towards the entrance. They turned and waved goodbye to her before reluctantly entering the building. As they walked towards their classroom, they could hear the booming voice of Mr Rehmani echoing down the hall. They knew they were late because he had already started to recite the Arabic alphabet.

"Girls, you are finally here!" The tall, bearded Persian teacher interrupted himself as he noticed them sneaking into the class. "Please find yourselves a seat in the quietest manner possible."

The small classroom had two long tables, one for the boys, the other for the girls. Farina and Imrana, intimidated by the teacher, quickly found themselves two empty seats on the girls' side. Sabrina, not scared of adults, slowly scanned the room for a good seat. There was an empty chair at the boys' table, right next to Ali, a cute boy who the girls knew from school. Sabrina fixed her eyes on that seat. The girls nervously fixed their eyes on her. Would she dare to sit with the boys? Without thinking too hard about it, Sabrina went and plonked herself down right next to Ali.

"No!" Mr Rehmani's sudden loud voice startled the kids. "Sister, you can't do that. You can't sit with the brothers!"

Farina and Imrana burst out laughing. Sabrina looked at them and grinned slyly. Some of the other girls also smiled but the boys looked down at their laps, showing off their discipline. Ali looked more offended than flattered.

"Get off the chair, get off the chair!" Mr Rehmani forced Sabrina to leave her seat. He angrily moved the chair over to the girls' table and wagged his finger at her. "Never do that again, sister!"

"Sorry, sir." Sabrina was happy that he had placed her chair next to Imrana's. "I'll never do it again."

The teacher sighed and wiped off drops of sweat from his forehead with his sleeve. "You girls stop laughing so we can get back to learning."

"Sorry, sir."

Farina, Sabrina, and Imrana couldn't stop their giggling and the teacher decided to ignore them and continued with his Arabic lesson. He placed his pointer on the first of a string of letters that were neatly written out on the blackboard.

"Repeat after me: 'Alif'!"

The class resounded with an enthusiastic *"Alif!"*

"Baa!"

"Baa!"

The teacher turned to the blackboard to point at the third letter of the alphabet when a girl bleated "Baa-a-a-a."

"Someone dares bleating in my class?" the teacher bellowed. He scanned the shocked faces at the boys' table, expecting one of the boys to be the troublemaker. A girlish giggle switched his attention to the girls' table.

He shifted his glare from Sabrina to Imrana and finally to Farina. All three had turned red from suppressing their laughter. He knew that one of the three pests had to be the culprit. He didn't care who it was as long as he could discipline one of them to set an example. He chose Farina.

Mr Rehmani walked slowly towards Farina, one long leg dragging behind the other. Farina stopped laughing now. Sabrina and Imrana shut up too; they were scared for their friend.

The teacher placed his large hands on the table. He stopped until his eyes were level with Farina's. "My little sister, why do you disturb my class?"

"I-I didn't mean to, sir." Farina looked at him ashamedly. If she didn't love Sabrina so very much, she would've told the teacher that it was Sabrina who had disturbed his class.

"My dear, do you not appreciate this opportunity to learn about your religion? To learn about Allah?"

"I do, sir!"

"Tell me something, sister, where are you from?"

"Bangladesh, sir."

"Bangladesh! There are a lot of brothers and sisters there, did you know that?" The teacher looked around the class to make sure that all his pupils were paying attention.

"Yes, sir. My mom told me."

"Did you also know that Bangladesh is one of the poorest countries in the world? Children your age have nothing there, but they still have the will to pray to Allah. Children there will beg for food on the streets, but they will never forget Allah!"

Farina didn't say anything. She felt sorry for those children that she'd never met.

"They don't have toys. They play marbles with the seeds of fruit. They are lucky if they have two pairs of clothes. Many of them will go years wearing the same shirt and pants. How many shirts do you have, sister?"

Farina began to sniffle. "I have many shirts, sir."

"Of course you do, sister. You don't live in your parents' country where children are happy just to afford a Quran! And you're a *sister*; the most horrible things happen to girls in poor countries. But they remain wrapped in their veils because they are good Muslims! Even through all their suffering, they remember their duty to Allah!"

Farina, heavy with guilt, managed to utter through her sobs, "So why can't Allah help my sisters?"

"Allah does help your sisters! No matter how poor and hungry they are, they are still promised their place in Jannah!" Mr Rehmani strolled around the class now, making contact with every remorseful pair of eyes, especially the ones at the girls' table. "Now look at you girls. You have everything you need and so much more, but what does all that mean if your afterlife is doomed?"

Farina sobbed loudly and called out to the teacher, "I'm sorry I disturbed your class, sir!"

Mr Rehmani leaned into Farina again. He began to whisper something he didn't intend for the rest of the class to hear: "You disturb my class because you have no respect for your roots, sister. I know very well you and your friends' type. You will grow up to walk around the malls all day in your tight clothes. You will have as many boyfriends as you like. You will neglect your books and party instead."

"No, I love books, sir," Farina insisted. "I love reading. I love writing. I want to be a poet one day."

"There is no place for poets left in your materialistic world," the teacher chuckled patronizingly. "Trust me, you will lose your way. Do you know why?"

Farina shook her head despondently.

"Because you live here, not in Bangladesh, or Iran, or Somalia: you are free to do whatever you desire! Sisters have freedom here, don't they?"

Farina took a second to think about her teacher's question. Freedom was a good thing. Her mother must've brought her here because there's more good here than where she was born. Her mother would only want the best for her. Without a doubt in her mind, she nodded, "Yes, we are free here."

"You will change your mind soon, little girl! You're only free in the West to be as immoral as the men who exploit you. You're free to give into lust and greed—things that do nothing to better this world. You're free to lose your passion and your compassion—the only things that make humans human." Mr Rehmani took a deep breath and paused before finishing with Farina: "My dear little sister, you won't realize the falsehood of this liberation until you're shackled by your own self-contempt."

Mr Rehmani's words were much too complicated for seven-year-old Farina to understand. Rather than contemplating anything he said, she looked over his shoulder to see how her friends were reacting. Imrana sat still with tears streaming down her face. Sabrina did not look as affected. She smiled flirtatiously at the boys, playing with the rings on her fingers as the teacher continued with his lesson.

ONE

May, 2001

I know it's dangerous for a girl to strut around the Eastside this late. And that's why I'm so happily doing it.

After a good hour or so of taking in the cool midnight air, I start to go back home. With my feet in high heels and my lips around a cigarette, I intentionally pass through the worst street of the ghetto. This is the place where all the junkies buy their candy and all the hookers sell their love. Such a paranoid and delusional bunch doesn't like to see a new face in their shop. If it's trouble you want, you just have to show up here.

Unfortunately, the potholed street is nearly empty tonight. Except for a hunched figure stading at the far corner, there's nobody to thrill me. As I come closer to it, I can tell it's an older woman. As soon as she hears the sound of my heels, she turns to look at me. Her bright lipstick and tacky dress tell me that she's a hooker. Definitely not a successful one considering she has hair like wet fur and more wrinkles on her face than a bulldog. She stands as still as the lamppost beside her. Her beady eyes glare at me from underneath her red bangs. With one hand hidden in her purse, she flashes me a toothless but menacing grin.

My strides get shorter. I wanted this. I wanted to see the East-side at night. All by myself. Until tonight, I'd never seen the world alone after ten o'clock. I was so excited about it. I thought about this stupid walk all day at work. I was supposed to get into a dangerous but harmless adventure and then tell Sabrina and Imrana all about it. But now I'm about to be pepper-sprayed by some hooker. Or maybe stabbed. Or maybe shot.

I can run back and take the safer road home, but that's out of question. That's exactly what my mother would want me to do. I'm done listening to her. I'm going to walk right past the old whore no matter what she pulls out.

I take a drag on my cigarette and follow the dense smoke as it slowly escapes my mouth. I shift my stare from the smoke to the cigarette to my feet as I approach the woman. My eyes won't let me confront hers. I wish I had the courage to meet them and invite a fight. If I weren't a brown girl, I wouldn't have to think twice about it. None of the black or white girls in this neighbourhood have been told since birth to be "perfect." They don't have Aunties and Uncles watching everything they do either.

I can see from the corner of my eye the old hooker's hand emerging from her purse. My heart pounds as she extends her hand to me. I pause, and dare to look at what she's holding.

It's just a business card.

"Here you go, sweetie," she gives me the card and whispers, "Jesus is with you tonight."

At the top of the card there's a cartoon of a crying circus elephant. Underneath there's a caption: ARE YOU TIRED OF TURNING TRICKS? CALL THE CHURCH EMPLOYMENT CENTRE TODAY.

I give her the card back and snap, "I'm not a hooker."

"Sorry, dear!" Her cheeks flush. "You should go home then. Only wicked girls walk the streets at night. People will get ideas."

"You don't look so holy standing around here either." I flick my cigarette away and quickly continue on my way home—this was more than enough excitement for the night.

The droning of crickets follows me all the way to Peckville. I arrive at a block, at one end of which stands a much-too-familiar apartment building. Here is where my parents live. I search the tall columns of windows until I find the one with turquoise curtains and a row of fern on the sill. All the lights are on so they must be awake and fighting. I wish they'd look out the window for a second. I'm sure that my dad would ignore me, but my mom would absolutely lose her mind. I'd love to see her face when she recognizes me out here in the dark wearing nothing but tight jeans and a tank top. Then I'd like to shout out to her at the top of my voice: "What are you going to do now, Mom? You can't lock up your little girl anymore, can you? You can't do shit!"

She really can't do shit. In this wonderful country, whether you're a boy or a girl, you belong to yourself once you turn eighteen. I turned eighteen seven months ago and immediately began to plan my freedom. I got a job at Nelly's Deli and started to put away for my own place. To save myself from a good beating, I decided to move out first and then drop out of university. To make sure that my mom didn't hold me back with tears or with force, I packed my stuff secretly, little by little, and left while she was at work. Two weeks ago. I'm free now.

The only thing that I forgot to include in my perfect plan was a scheme to get rich. I'm still stuck in Peckville because it's all I can afford. I'm not nearly far enough away from all the preaching and gossiping Bangladeshis. I'm definitely not far enough away from my parents. Just one building away, to be exact.

ↄ

I see my new neighbour standing in front of his apartment. He's rummaging through his pockets, probably searching for his keys. If he doesn't want to knock on the door and wake his parents up, he's more than welcome to spend the night in my bed.

I don't pay much attention to brown boys, but this one is hard to overlook. He's just as dirt-poor as the rest of them, but he looks better than any of the rich haircuts and suits downtown. He's tall and lean with the smoothest almond-coloured skin and the thickest black hair. His cheekbones and his jawlines are sharp enough to cut glass. His deep-set dark eyes and his childlike smile are just something else. I've always thought so.

His name is Ali and I've known him ever since elementary school. We didn't speak much then and we didn't speak at all during high school. There, he was loved for being on the basketball team and always making the honour roll. I was hated for hanging out with Sabrina and always sleeping with somebody's boyfriend. I made the honour roll too, but never bothered to show up at the award ceremonies. He also had his share of rebellious friends, but that only made him cooler because he's a boy. His popularity and my infamy stopped us from talking to each other back then, no matter how many times our eyes locked in the main hallway.

I guess we'll always simply lock eyes in a hallway and nothing else because we still don't talk. He half-smiles at me before he finally finds his keys and disappears into his apartment. I'm sure that his hijab-wearing mother has already warned him about the slut next door.

Every time I enter my new home, all I can think about is that I need a drink. There is no place more depressing than this rat hole. The white paint on the living-room walls is peeling off and reveals a disgusting pastel yellow. The crevices behind the paint have become dwellings for cockroaches, ants, and insects I don't even know the names of. Both the bedroom and the washroom door are dented as if someone swung a bat into them. There's a red stain on the bedroom door; I'm more than sure that it's some poor soul's blood. The kitchen smells worse than the mouldy washroom and none of their faucets have hot water after midnight. And as if all that weren't enough, the uncarpeted floor is too cold to walk on without socks because the superintendent is too cheap to turn the heat on. I guess I'm paying nine hundred bucks a month for shelter and shelter alone.

The only pleasing sight in my apartment is my collection of books. All my favourite novels and poetry compilations are stacked together on the floor because I can't afford a bookcase, but I still feel a little peace when I look at them. I stopped reading years ago, but I retain secret passion for literature. I really don't believe in anything but the power of words and God. Lately, I'm not too sure about the latter.

I walk to the kitchen, my hands idly hooked around my neck. I open the cupboard door above the sink and go through its contents like a hungry racoon exploring the inside of a trashcan. A plastic jar of salt comes rolling down somehow, hitting the top of my head before the floor and losing its lid. I'll clean the salt off of the floor tomorrow morning. Yeah, that will be the highlight of my Saturday. Behind the large box of cereal that my mom left me four days ago, I find my precious bottle of vodka.

The reason I keep my alcohol in the back of my cabinet and not somewhere within easy reach is because my mom could barge in here anytime. She can't know that I drink. Good Muslim girls don't drink alcohol. They don't smoke weed or fuck before marriage either. Not being much of a good Muslim girl, I don't follow any of those three rules, but I'll always be a coward and pretend like I do in front of my mom. Although I love pissing her off, I really hate seeing her cry.

I bring the bottle and the cleanest glass I can find to the living room. The air in this apartment is frigid as usual and it chills the walls, the furniture, and the clothes on the floor, which I haven't yet had time to fold. Maybe I'll get lucky and freeze to death one of these nights. Maybe, when my frozen corpse makes the evening news, I'll finally be famous. Maybe then, once my parents realize that I died living on my own, they'll regret driving me out of their place with their backward rules.

I won't be that lucky though. Dying isn't easy.

Thoughts of death run through my mind a lot lately; probably because I don't have a TV. I've never been and still am not a fan of what Mr TV has to say, but at least his senseless chatter would make me feel like I'm still a part of the world. Right now, I feel like

I'm living in a perpetual state of death. How can you exist to the world if the world doesn't exist to you? I have no idea what's going on out there. And nobody knows or cares what's going on in here.

I down a glass of the vodka and find my cellphone to keep myself busy. There are five missed calls and two voice messages. One of the calls is from Imrana and, as I expected, four are from my mom. I toss the phone down on the seat while the voicemail plays on speaker mode. I pour myself another glass of vodka and smile with relief as the alcohol tickles the back of my throat.

The first message is from my mom. Her English is laced with the same Bengali accent she had years ago. The only noticeable improvement is her grammar. I shut my eyes tightly as the whole apartment fills with her calm voice:

"Hello? Farina? It's your mom. You didn't call me or your father today and you said you would. So I was worried, and that's why I called. I miss you . . . so does your father. It's Friday; you don't have work tomorrow, why don't you sleep here with us tonight? You don't even have to talk to us if you don't want to. Just sleep in your bed, ok? Give me a call back soon. Bye."

Fourteen days with no leash around my neck is too much for my mom to handle. She calls me every day and begs me to come back. She has always thought and still thinks that I'm such a fuck-up that unless she watches and guides my every little move, I will fuck something up. But I know that she wants me back with her not only because of safety reasons. She's horrified about the ridiculous rumours that our Bangladeshi neighbours are spreading about me. I'm now the unmarried girl who left my parents to live with my drug-dealing boyfriend. I'm also the dropout who gave it all up to become a movie star.

My mother works hard at upholding an ideal image of our family. She wants to convince all the Aunties and Uncles that her household is perfectly functional. No, we have not fallen victim to the daily pressures that this country casts upon its immigrants. We're still a pious and traditional Bangladeshi family. She's the housewife who happily cleans and cooks for her husband and child. My father is the great provider who assures the prosperity of his family and the functionality of its members. I'm the obedient daughter who studies all the time, loves to help my mother around the house, and wishes only to be some rich doctor's wife one day. Bullshit.

My mother is a liar. Although I miss her, I'm in no mood to call her.

I pour myself another drink as Imrana's message follows a beep:

"Rina, I'm coming upstairs to see you. I'm going to sneak out when my parents fall asleep so expect me to be there around one— and dress up."

Dress up? Maybe tonight's the night that Sabrina's finally throwing me a party for my new apartment. She congratulated me a million times over the phone, but she hasn't come down to see the place yet. Come to think of it, she hasn't come to see me ever since she mysteriously moved out of Peckville a few months ago. She didn't even invite me to her and her mother's new condo. I really hope I see her tonight because I have a lot of questions lined up.

I look at the time on my cell phone. It's ten minutes past one, so punctual Imrana should be here any minute now. The thought of getting ready to go out sends a rush of energy and exhilaration through me. Doing my hair and putting make-up on excites me now the same way that doodling did when I was a nerdy little kid. Maybe that's because the mixing of colourful eye shadows is the only creative activity I get these days. Or maybe not—what do I know? I'm just an insignificant little Paki girl.

After a good long stretch, I collect my make-up and place myself in front of the large mirror in the washroom. Thanks to a year of university and all its fine-printed books, my hooded eyes look tired. Other than that, I look as good as I always did. I got my mom's squared face, her hazel eyes, her plump lips, and her light skin. Nobody would ever guess that I'm brown, but I have my dad's hooked nose. The worst part of me came from my father.

After touching up my face and brushing my long highlighted hair, I return to the living room to fill my fourth glass of vodka. My glass in my hand, I search through the pile of clothes on the floor to find something to wear. My mom would always buy me whatever clothes I wanted as long as they covered most of my skin and distorted all of my curves. Obviously, I have very few clothes that would impress at a party. I only have two dresses and they were both gifts from Sabrina. One is a little piece of stretchy red cloth that has no straps and is so tight that it outlines my nipples. The other is a low-cut, classy little black dress. I decide to go with the black one just because it's more proper.

On second thoughts, I choose the red one. There's nobody around to dictate what's proper or improper anymore.

Just as I take off my jeans and tank top, I hear a swift knock on the door. I quickly step into the red dress and pull it up high enough to bare a little cleavage. I find my heels and strap them on clumsily. I quickly take a look at the finished me in the washroom. I definitely look a lot better than I feel.

Ready for compliments, I open the door with a big smile— which quickly turns into a puzzled frown when I see Imrana in her flannel pyjamas. She's wearing a pair of furry slippers and holding a large gym bag. Her wavy black hair is tied back into a bun and there's nothing on her round face except for lip gloss.

"Why aren't you dressed? You can't go out like that."

"I didn't say we're going out." Imrana grins, showing off her bottomless dimples.

It's impossible to be upset with Imrana when she smiles. When those dimples emerge on her face, I forget that she's just as big a bitch as Sabrina and me. All I remember is the chocolate-skinned girl that Sabrina and I'd always protect in elementary school. I remember the mean Paki boys calling her "darkie." A few of them, the ones who understood rap, called her "nigger." Whenever I caught a boy teasing her I'd hold him down while Sabrina stomped on his immature dick. Although Imrana's a few months older than me, I always think of her as my baby sister.

I calm down and shut the door after her. "So why did you tell me to dress up?"

"I'm gonna tell you in a minute." Imrana finds my vodka bottle on the table and doesn't hesitate to help herself.

That bottle of vodka is costing me a week of no chicken or cheese. My lousy job at the deli pays just enough for rent, basic groceries, and phone bills. To afford alcohol, I have to cut into my food budget. I might get my legs broken for the rent and the phone bill, but nobody will care if I eat or not. I care a lot though. My parents weren't so great with love and all that mushy stuff, but they always fed me good. I'm not used to crackers and jam for every meal of the day. I feel a sudden rage as I watch Imrana chugging down the vodka like it was free.

I grab the bottle from her and whine, "Don't fucking finish it."

"No need to be a greedy bitch." She drops into my couch and pats her gym bag. "Bringing you more vodka is the reason I'm here."

She smirks, pulling out a tall bottle from her bag. It's a frosted bottle with that distinctive shape and crystal-studded emblem. If my eyes aren't fooling me, then it's the most expensive brand of vodka available.

"This is why I told you to dress up." Imrana holds up the bottle with both hands like it's an offering to the heavens.

"They put these behind locked doors." I take the bottle and marvel at the crystals. "How'd you get away with stealing it?"

"I didn't steal it. I didn't buy it either. Sabrina came to campus today and told me to give it to you. She said it's for your 'new found freedom'."

I raise a brow. "How the hell did she afford this?"

"I guess the bank pays really good." Imrana shrugs. "Who cares?

I had my last exam today, let's just get drunk."

I screw the cap off with my teeth and sigh with satisfaction before taking a sip. For the first time in my life, I taste the alcohol of the rich and relevant. Surprisingly, it tastes identical to my usual brand. But there's something magical about holding this jewelled bottle in my hand. I don't feel like myself. I feel like somebody much better.

Imrana drinks my cheap vodka. She reaches into her gym bag and brings out something else. She drops a bunch of plastic pawns on the table and reaches into her bag again.

"Chess, Imrana? Really?"

"What do you want to do all night? You ain't got a TV."

She's got a point. I sit next to her as she organizes the pieces on the board.

I warn her, "Just don't tell anybody about this."

Imrana nods in agreement. "How's the deli going?"

"It's hell. I'm gonna find something else to do really soon."

"It's funny that you say that because Sabrina actually wants us to visit her at work on Monday night. She said she has a business proposal to discuss with us."

I stare at Imrana, curious to know whether she's kidding or not. She looks at me and drinks nonchalantly as if she hadn't just said something completely ridiculous.

I turn the chessboard so that the white pieces are mine and ask dryly, "What kinda business are we gonna run? A blowjob stand?"

"Probably," Imrana laughs. "You know how crazy Sabrina is."

TWO

Clint Merlon, my manager at Nelly's Deli, called me earlier this morning and begged me to come in. Although my head was throbbing from all the alcohol I had last night, I decided to do him this favour. Well, I'm not really doing him a favour since I need the overtime pay desperately. And I'd rather be downtown working than moping around in that goddamn apartment.

Because it's close to noon, the time of day when the largest delivery comes in, I enter the store through its backdoor. It would spare me a good minute if I used the front, but I don't want to miss the delivery boys. I like to strut by them while they're all working together: men are the manliest when other males are around. They're bound to notice me and make it clear when they do. Although I'm not very interested in any of them, I want a little of their attention before I start work. Their stares and whispers add some excitement to the boring day. More importantly, it reminds me that I'm still visible, desirable. I'm not fading away behind the fog of the deli counter. I haven't been kidnapped yet by the working world.

The store is packed with customers. Anyone who isn't making money on a sunny Saturday is out spending it. I wish I was one of them instead of serving them. Seeing the carefree grins on their tanned faces as they come by in their shorts and sandals pisses me off. After they're done buying their sandwiches or whatever, they'll go to the beach. They'll spend the whole day there lazing under the sun while I'll be here, sweating under the blinding fluorescent lights. Maybe I should've stayed home. Yeah, I should've stayed home and thought of a better way to pay the fucking bills.

I dash upstairs and decide to waste some time in Clint's office. Of course, a lot of perks come with flirting with your boss, but I don't just flirt with Clint because I like the longer breaks and phone privileges. He's a very good-looking man. And because his daddy owns this store and several others, he's also quite rich. It'd be nice to know him outside of work. I'm sure he'd give me a lot more rewards if nobody was looking. Too bad we have nothing in common except for a lust for the forbidden. Too bad he'd never invite me and my cheap clothes to his uptown mansion. Really too bad he's thirty-five and married.

I lean against the doorframe of his office, my arms crossed under my breasts to create a deep cleavage. It doesn't take long for Clint to shift his bright blue eyes from his monitor to me.

"How are you, Farina? Thanks for coming in. I missed you." He scans me from head to toe.

He looks as sharp as usual in a fitted striped shirt, sleek dress pants, and black leather derbies. I always notice what he's wearing because it's never the same outfit twice.

I smile at him suggestively. "I only came because I missed you."

Thinking he'll want to inquire why I missed him, I stupidly make myself comfortable in the chair across his desk.

"Now don't sit down—it's a storm downstairs. You gotta get working."

He swiftly returns to his screen, pretending he has no interest in me. Nothing comes before business.

I wait a second for him to say something, but he doesn't. I watch the gold on his ring finger gleam with every movement as he types away on his keyboard. I don't feel like going downstairs yet. I want to be up here just a little bit longer. I want to be close to Clint's clean designer clothes and expensive scent just a little bit longer.

"I'm so tired," I sigh. "I think I had a little too much last night."

Clint's interested again. "You like to drink?"

"I love to drink." I cross my fingers for an invitation.

"Well, you never told me that before." He stops typing and gives me his undivided attention. His deep eyes penetrate into mine, looking far past his monitor and the picture of his wife next to it.

"Is that a thing to tell your boss?" I twirl a strand of hair around my finger.

"I'm not just your boss, am I?" Clint retracts into his leather chair with a confident smile on his handsome face. "Tell me, what else do you love to do?"

I plaster an equally confident smile on my face. "Buy me lunch and I'll tell you."

Clint laughs. "Sure, I'll buy you lunch. Not here though—we'll say we're delivering an order and take my car somewhere."

"Which one did you bring today?"

"The black Mercedes."

I bite my lower lip to contain my excitement. I've never been in an expensive car before. The guys that Sabrina, Imrana and I used to ride with were poor losers in their parents' sedans. A few of them could afford a cool paint job, but the flashy colours only attracted more attention to the sputtering engines.

"I'll be taking my lunch in two hours." I slap my thighs and jump up happily.

"I'll come down and check on you soon." Clint scans my body one last time before returning to his work.

As he sits back into his leather chair, he runs his fingers through his flaxen hair. His gelled bangs point upwards, shining like a gold crown on his head.

Through the glass door of the staff lunchroom, I notice that the only person sitting there is the old caretaker. His wrinkled lips are so fine that his mouth looks like a scabbed gash from afar. I can't remember if his name's Ben or Ken. He's never said a word to me. All I know about him is that he sucks at his job. The lunchroom is filthy.

My locker door makes a loud squeak as I fling it open. The only things inside are my uniform and a magnetic mirror. My uniform consists of a pair of black shoes, a pair of black dress pants, a white shirt, and an apron with Nelly's Deli basil leaf logo on it. I wouldn't look too bad in the uniform if I wasn't forced to wear a hairnet with it. Nobody can make a hairnet look good.

The caretaker's so focused on his newspaper that I don't mind changing right in front of him. Even if he took a peek at my peach-coloured panties, I wouldn't be too angry with him. He doesn't have too many years left so let him have whatever little thrills he can get. I have a lot of pity for the old man. While we're both here, working mindlessly for peanuts, I have the advantage of time. I'm still young enough to wait for something else to come along. The only thing coming to save poor Ben or Ken from this sad, sad place is death.

The hags throw a lazy "hello" my way as I come downstairs and step behind the counter. There are six of them on shift today. There's no point in me describing each one of them because they're pretty much interchangeable. They're all in their late thirties or early forties, terrible with English, moody, loud, and disgustingly fat.

Before one of the hags can tell me what to do, I make my way over to the meat-slicing machine. My usual task is to slice meat, pack meat, and serve meat. Slice meat, pack meat, serve meat. For eight hours. On my aching feet. Sometimes, when I'm lucky, I get to stick some of that meat into a sandwich. Those times are rare because everyone else wants to make and serve the sandwiches. Making sandwiches does require a bit of thought.

The sandwich line is so long that I can hardly make out the patient sucker at the very end. Four of the hags are sweating with the orders, one is refilling the condiments, and the last one is parked at my station.

I poke Paullina gently on her back and try to speak over the chatty mob. "I'm here; you can do something else now!"

Paullina snarls at me. "No, I'm doing fine here! You go help with sandwiches!"

No, she's not doing fine at all. There are salami and prosciutto pieces stuck to the blade and to her gloves. The next Jew who wants chicken is going to get pissed. But of course Paullina doesn't care about that as long as she gets to avoid the rush of customers.

I can't really blame her for wanting to avoid them. The customers are the worst part about working at Nelly's Deli. They're not the kids you see at burger joints whose only complaint is that their fries aren't salty enough. Because the deli is in the richest part of downtown, half of the customers are important suits with very short fuses. The other half is of course their wives and girlfriends. They're all demanding snobs who are so used to getting their way that they throw tantrums over tiny mistakes. Some of them like to snap their fingers at you when you're not going fast enough. Some like to scream at you if you forget to include a napkin. A few like to hurl their sandwich back in your face if they aren't happy with it.

The drama never ends when the poor are tossed against the rich.

I'm too hung-over to start a fight so I decide to let Paullina have my station. I don't mind dealing with customers as much as she does. Unlike everyone else here, I'm a lot more fascinated by the rich than I am intimidated. The women, especially, are something to be amazed by.

The woman next in line is no exception. Just like the rest of them, she's got a pretty face, a tiny waist, and a suit with his arm around her. Her complexion, like varnished leather, is as flawless as her manicured nails and freshly done hair. Her clothes and jewellery, too unique to be cheap, are carefully matched in every chromatic detail. Her purse, worth more than two months of my rent, hangs off of her proud, broad shoulder. With an appearance as impressive as hers, it's no wonder that she stands with her lips puckered, her head up, and her fake breasts way out.

But it's not her appearance that makes me watch her with bittersweet admiration. It's her endless resources of time and dime. To look beautiful perpetually requires a bottomless wallet and little responsibility for anyone but yourself. While women like my mother work all day, first for her boss and then for my father, these women spend their energies only at malls and spas. They didn't have to drain their spirits at university to get where they are; they just had to keep fit and spread their legs. They're the real winners of the race. They can do whatever they want. They're free.

The suit smiles at me before he says to his girlfriend, "What do you want to eat, honey?"

The woman whispers something quietly in his ear. She doesn't smile or even look at me once. Either I'm invisible or she's so used to getting everything through her man that he mediates between her and the world. Or maybe she's just having an awful day. What do I know? I'm just a little insignificant Paki girl.

He orders turkey on focaccia as the woman steps aside and answers her cellphone. She turns around and I find myself checking out the embellished back of her designer jeans. While I wait for Paullina to pass me the turkey, I wonder if I'll ever be able to own a pair of jeans like that. I imagine myself seven years down the road, no longer a teenager but a full-grown twenty-five-year-old, strutting around in outfits like that. How sweet life would be if I had money when Ali and all the other "smart" Bangladeshis from Peckville were worrying about their student loans.

All those Aunties and Uncles couldn't call me a loser anymore if I was rich. Well, they wouldn't even know about me because I'd move far away from Peckville. Yeah, I'd buy a big condo close to the clubbing district and have Sabrina and Imrana live with me. We'd get drunk and high every night. My mother would feel dumb for thinking that I'd never make it on my own. She'd have to apologize for treating me like a little girl. She'd have to respect me. Maybe even be proud of me.

I snap out of my dream as Paullina slaps down the turkey slices in front of me. With very little enthusiasm, I ask the suit, "What do you want on the sandwich, sir?"

He glances at his girlfriend who's still chatting away on her phone, then decides to guess what she wants. He hesitates a lot with his choices as if he's frightened of making the wrong one: "Um . . . let's start with mayo . . . add some lettuce . . . um . . . a little cu-cucumber, maybe . . . and a few slices of cheddar, please."

I add everything on neatly and begin to wrap the sandwich when the woman returns from her phone call. She locks arms with the man and whispers into his ear again. His eyes widen and he nearly screams at me, "I forgot tomatoes!"

I keep my head down as I roll my eyes and undo the sandwich. The woman finally talks to me when I add the tomatoes.

"Is that mayonnaise?" Her face scrunches up with disgust.

"Yes."

"What type is it?"

"It's just regular mayo, ma'am." I notice the angry face of the next customer and begin wrapping the sandwich again.

The woman gives her man a cold look and then motions for me to stop. "I can't have that, sorry."

Not sure what to do, I stare at her dumbly, the wrapped sandwich in my hand. It's easy to just toss a sandwich and make a new one when nobody's around, but I'm surrounded by the hags right now. If they see me throwing a sandwich, they won't just tell Clint but also Clint's dad, the owner. There's nothing they love more than ratting out other workers. It makes their pathetic selves feel powerful.

"Do you want me to wipe off the mayo?" I ask the woman half-sarcastically.

The man finally interrupts, "I'll have that sandwich, please make a new one for her."

"No, you just ate." The woman gives the man another cold

look. She turns to me and insists, "Just get me another one with fat-free mayo."

I could just tell the little queen that we don't have fat-free mayo, but I'd rather just piss her off some more. I say with my most hospitable smile, "I can get you another sandwich, but you'll have to go to the back of the line."

The woman's face isn't so pretty anymore. "Excuse me?"

"I'm sorry, ma'am, but people are waiting. You have to go to the back of the line."

She nods to her boyfriend like you would signal your dog to attack. His face goes red. "Either make us our sandwich or we'll have a chat with your manager, sweetheart."

"What's going on here?" One of the hags, an Eastern European psychopath named Olga, decides to intervene and make me look incompetent. "How can I help you, sir?"

"Your employee here messed up our order and refuses to make us another sandwich." The man glares at me contemptuously, along with Olga and every other customer in line. "I wouldn't expect this kind of service here."

Olga and the other hags look at me for an answer. I stay quiet and don't bother to defend myself. It's a goddamn sandwich. I don't give a fuck about a stupid sandwich. I got bills to pay. Fuck them. Fuck them all.

But I'd be lying if I said that I'm not a bit embarrassed. Unless it's because I look good, I don't like having so many eyes on me. I switch my gaze from the ceiling to the floor to the walls, trying my best to avoid eye contact with anyone right now. But suddenly there's a person in the room that I can't help but lock eyes with.

"Well, what do you have to say for yourself, Farina?" Olga asks me like she's a judge or something.

Not moving my eyes from that conspicuous person in faded jeans and an old blouse, I talk to the air, "Excuse me, I'm going to the washroom."

I can hear Olga's shrieking voice calling my name as I leave the counter for the back room. I don't care right now. All I can think about is that my mother is here.

I pace back and forth in the empty room, completely confused as to what I should feel. I'm angry that she dared to track me down at work, but I missed her so much that I'm also happy. I only have a few seconds to decide on a reaction before she storms in here and decides my feelings for me. A smoke could really help calm my nerves right now. I find a cigarette in my pocket—but instead of lighting it, I flick it away. I can't smoke in front of my mom.

When she finally walks through the door, I only feel one thing: fear. I'm petrified that I don't recognize any of the wrinkles on her face. She didn't look this old two weeks ago. Maybe she did look this old, but I didn't notice because I'd seen her the day before, and the day before that day. Those wrinkles on her face wouldn't be so scary if they had emerged in my presence. They wouldn't be omens of time passing away, but accolades of time spent together. I'm afraid now that I'm moving further away from her as she's moving closer to that final day. Maybe I did leave too soon.

All of a sudden, I feel a strong urge to just hold her tight and not let go. I'd love to go back to those years when I was barely tall enough to reach her waist. I wouldn't have to bend my back to hug her then; I'd rest my head on her soft stomach and lose myself in the security of her arms. Life was an easy ride back then. Bills were magically taken care of and food just appeared on the table. Sure, my father was still screaming all the time and I was forced to be a "proper" girl, but I was too young to complain. I was too naïve to be angry.

"You can't even call us?" she shoots out in Bengali before hugging me. There's no warmth in her embrace. "Do you know how worried your father was? We could not sleep for two days! We thought you tried to cook something and blew up the oven instead! We thought you were dead!"

Of course she thought that I was dead. Of course I'm so incredibly stupid that I'd somehow cause the oven to explode. Suddenly I'm not so nostalgic or panicked by my mother's mortality. Just for a minute, I forgot about her low opinion of me. I forgot that I'll never be good enough in her eyes unless I chase her dreams, believe in her beliefs, and behave according to her standards. I forgot the very reason I left her in the first place.

"Your father is outside; after you're finished with work, we're going to help you pack your stuff—you're coming home tonight," my mom says as if it's a sure fact.

Of course my father couldn't bother to come in to see me. I wouldn't expect him to. He likes to outsource all of his responsibilities to my mother—especially the one of parenting.

My mom doesn't look the slightest bit worried that I might refuse to go back with her. She still thinks that she can tell me what to do. She hasn't grasped the fact yet that I'm an adult with rights. I feel a familiar rage boiling inside me. It's the same one that appeared every time I was barred from going to a party, interrogated for having a male friend, or forced to cover my ankles.

"I'm not going anywhere," I reply in English and grind my teeth. "You have some nerve coming all the way down here."

This is the awkward way in which we always talk. She yaks in Bengali, a language I find easy to understand but impossible to speak; I snap back in English, a language she has no choice but to understand and no need to learn how to speak. They only need my mom to comprehend instructions at the factories—not to share her opinions or thoughts.

My mother throws her arms up in frustration. "What else do you want me to do? I've been calling, calling, calling, and you don't pick up—"

"And what if I wasn't at work? Where would you go to find me?"

She looks just as angry and offended as I am. "Where else would you be but at home or at work?"

"There are many places to be," I say daringly.

"Like where?" she shouts. The fear in her eyes is as authentic as the rage in her clenched fists.

"I don't have to tell you anything." I try to pass her and leave the room, but she grips my shoulders tightly.

"Don't forget who you are. Don't forget who we are," my mother whispers in order to contain the echo in the room. God forbid somebody hears us argue; keeping up appearances is always her top priority. "We are a good Muslim family. People respect your father and me. You may feel like we don't have much here, Farina, but in Bangladesh, it's a very different life. We have land, family, history, and everything is just for you."

I don't know why she's bringing up this faraway land that I don't remember and will never see again. Are all these fantastical things in Bangladesh just a bribe to keep me away from sex and alcohol? Well, it's too late for that.

"Mom, I've made my choice." I firmly remove her hand from my shoulder. "I'm never coming back."

My mom has spent so many years pretending that we're happy that she has come to forget reality. Her confusion is sincere when she asks me, "Why, Farina? Don't you know that if you stray too far from your origin, you get lost forever? Why do you never want to come back to your own mother?"

She hasn't asked me this question yet in the past two weeks and I haven't bothered to come up with a clear answer for it. I never discuss my problems with her. There's no point really because she never sees her part in any of them. To my mother, all my problems are my own creations: simple knots in my life that I complicated with my lack of intelligence or my rejection of Islamic guidance. Nobody else is ever at fault—especially not she or my father.

But if she really wants to know what she has done wrong, I won't hesitate to tell her. I don't care anymore if she understands it or not. She's not a part of my new beginning. Feeling relaxed,

I say very frankly, "I hate how you think you own me, I hate how you don't let me go anywhere but school, and I hate—I absolutely hate—that you let Dad treat you like you're his slave! Maybe you're fine with somebody controlling every aspect of your life, Mom, but I'm not. I'm sorry, but I'm happy on my own."

I know I've said something disrespectful enough to earn a slap. I nearly flinch in the anticipation of one, but surprisingly, she doesn't look so appalled. She doesn't even look a little angry. She just laughs at me.

"What's so funny?"

"You're happy on your own, are you?" My mother grins at me derisively as she hands me an envelope from her purse. "Your bank statement came to us."

I'm not surprised to see that the envelope has been opened. My parents couldn't care less about my privacy rights. I remember having a big fight with her about the issue not long ago. She insisted that only shady people with secrets needed privacy—why should a good girl like me be allowed any?

"You are getting paid at the end of next week—what do you plan to eat until then? You don't have ten dollars and you're telling me that you're happy on your own?" My mother's face trembles as she fights to uphold her mocking smile. But she doesn't really want to smile.

The last thing I need is for someone to announce my financial situation to my face. It's a cancer I'd like to ignore. My sleepless nights are beginning to prove to me that the uncertainty and fear that come with having no money outweigh the pleasure of having complete independence. Unless I ignore the possibility of starving between paycheques, I'll forever consider crawling back to my father's door. And so I gather all my strength, forget the warning that my mother's just thrown in my face, and declare reassuringly, "I'm gonna be fine. I have enough food for the week. I have a very secure budget. May and June rents are already paid. All I have to do now is prepare for July. Yeah, I'm gonna be fine."

I'm lying through my teeth. I don't have enough food for the week and I won't ever unless I get a second job. After rent, credit card bill, cellphone bill, transit pass, and alcohol, I can hardly afford to feed myself. That's the scary, ugly, hard truth.

"Okay, Farina, you will be fine." My mother nods with me as tears run down her pained face. There is nothing more for her to do but to accept that I'm gone. There is nothing more for her to say but goodbye. Yet she stands still in front of me, refusing to walk away.

My heart breaks at the sight of my mom crying, but before I can calm her down the door swings open.

"Are you on your break, Farina?" Clint nods at my mom, not too interested in introducing himself.

My mom makes me promise that I'll pick up her calls. She quickly wipes her tears away and disappears back into the store. For once, I doubt her speediness has anything to do with hiding our imperfections from others. I think she's just well aware of how screwed I'll be if I lose this job. This mind-numbing, feet-hurting, peanut-paying job is my lifeline.

"Who was that?"

"Nobody," I say blankly and make my way to the door.

"Now wait a second—" Clint blocks my way "—I just got a customer complaint against you. You wanna tell me what happened?"

"No, Clint, I really don't," I answer sharply. I have way more important things to worry about than offending some suit and his bimbo. "Do you really want to talk and waste time? Or can I just continue my job?"

Clint sighs as he gently massages my shoulders and back. "You know I like and trust you, but I really need to get more professionalism from you, honey."

"Professionalism?" I raise my brows. "I serve meat for a living. You should just be grateful that I speak English."

Clint laughs as he digs his long fingers deep into my back. "Alright, I'll let you go this time. Are we still on for lunch?"

I surprise myself at finding that I'm not so enthusiastic about lunch anymore. A ride in a nice-looking car doesn't seem so exciting right now. Sure, I'd feel like somebody important in that car, but the car isn't mine. Clint isn't mine. Clint's money definitely isn't mine. Once the ride is over, I'll be back to poor, penniless Farina Farooki: the Peckville Paki with ten dollars at the bank.

"I'm not in the mood." I swing out of Clint's grip. "Maybe some other day."

I return to the deli where none of the hags bother to acknowledge me. Let them be like that. I don't need them to like me. I'll be gone anyway as soon as I get what I need.

And what I need is money.

THREE

I wake up to the wailing of police cars and ambulances.

Sirens aren't so exciting to someone who's lived in Peckville as long as I have. They are a part of the background noise, like the rattling of the subway trains that rush past every three or four minutes. Instead of running to the window to see who's getting arrested, I pat around under my pillow to find my cellphone. It's five in the afternoon.

A long, long time ago, I was eager to wake up as early as possible. It felt wrong to "waste" the day. I don't feel so guilty anymore if I spend more time asleep than awake. The longer I sleep the shorter the day is. The shorter the day is the shorter conscious life is. The shorter conscious life is the faster I can get the hell out of my misery.

These thoughts of death are always here these days. I'm not sure why, though. I have no wish to die. I'd never kill myself. No, I'd never give my parents the pleasure of seeing me lost to the world. Suicide is a loser's ultimate defeat. Only weak people kill themselves and the last thing I am is weak. In grade eleven, while we were both high as a kite, Sabrina carved me a tattoo right below my nape to remind me that I'm not weak. A tiny diamond. "Nothing is tougher than a diamond," she said as we promised each other that we'd never cry.

If my stomach wasn't growling, I'd choose to lie down here for another hour or two. I force myself up and stretch away my lethargy. I throw on a large t-shirt and sweatpants and drag myself to the kitchen. I should probably brush my teeth before digging them into food, but I'm pretty sure that I'm out of toothpaste. Another thing to buy.

I catch a whiff of a stench behind me and it kills my appetite. It's the brimming garbage, the smell is now so bad that I must take care of it. I hold my breath and tie the bag as a swarm of disappointed flies buzz away. You'd think I'm getting rid of a corpse. I use both hands to drag the massive bundle to the hall. For someone who owns so little, I sure have a lot to throw away.

There is no way I can lift this thing up to the chute without it coming right back at me. With all the strength in my arms, I swing the bag over me with my eyes closed. At least I won't get garbage juice in my eyes if the bag rips. Just as I expected, most of the bag hangs outside the chute and slowly begins to come down on me. I catch the bottom of the bag and push it up with all my might. It glides in easily with the help of another pair of hands.

"Thanks." I smile at Ali, breaking four years of silence.

"No problem." He smiles back at me.

He's wearing a black suit with a black shirt, and I'm wondering if I'm dreaming. I have never seen Ali in a suit or in anything formal. He probably wore one for prom, but I wouldn't know because my mom wouldn't let me go. I hate to admit it, but he looks just as cute in his regular clothes as he does in this fancy getup. Maybe even a little cuter. I think I actually like him more in one of his plain t-shirts and baggy jeans.

I have never been this close to Ali's face before. His dark amber eyes tell a lot more up-close than they do from afar. I know that he's seen too much for someone who's blind. He's aware that the world is full of scorpions and snakes, but he thinks he's immune to their venom. I guess life is rosy when you're a male in university and a regular celebrity in the local mosque. He's going places—and that includes Heaven.

Ali chuckles. "So you're my neighbour now?"

I study his strong jaw and its contrast with his delicate lips. I wish I could kiss him deeply. If I had the right amount of alcohol in me, I'd slide my tongue into his mouth without asking.

I laugh innocently. "I guess we're never getting rid of each other."

Ali smiles and nods in agreement. He scratches the back of his shaved head as he searches for what to say next. I'm sure he wants to tell me that I should get my ass back to my parents. All the Bangladeshis know by now that I "ran away" and most of them have made one of two choices. The ones who are obsessed with reputation have decided to treat me like a leper. The ones who are obsessed with tradition have decided to bring me back to my father's jurisdiction. Ali must be in the latter group since he's actually talking to me.

"Are you liking your new place?" he finally utters after a long silence.

"It's alright," I lie. Excited by his overpowering height, I can't help but blurt out, "You wanna come in and see it?"

He turns red and wide-eyed with shock. I guess it was stupid of me to ask such a question to a respected Muslim from the holier-than-thou club. He probably wants to scream "Whore!" and drag me by my hair right now. Whatever. I had to try.

He surprises me. "Yeah, alright, why not? But not today, though; I'm going to a wedding. My friends are all waiting downstairs."

"So that explains the suit." I sigh inwardly with disappointment. "Who's getting married?"

"I think you know her—remember Nabila from high school?"

I match the name to the face and shake my head in disapproval. "She's only nineteen and her parents are locking her up already?"

Ali looks at me like I'm the dumbest person he's ever met. He argues his opinion with great conviction. "She didn't get into any university and she can't work at Big Burger forever. The guy's not too old and he's got a safe job at a pharmacy. She got lucky if you ask me."

"Whatever you say." I shrug indifferently.

There's no point in arguing with guys like Ali about girls' right to be free. We'll never be equals in their eyes.

"Speaking of university, I hear that you decided to leave?" Ali asks with a touch of scorn in his voice.

"Yep." I beam proudly and retort, "I hear that you decided to stay."

Ali pauses a second. Then nods briefly before making a gesture towards his apartment, where his parents are. "Do I really have a choice?"

I could of course say yes and tell him all about the joys of freedom, but I know that he'd just be offended. The last thing I want is to offend him and blow all my chances of getting into his pants. I decide to keep my mouth shut.

Ali pulls his brooding eyes away from me and glances at his watch. "I better go now."

He flaunts his cute smile before he turns around and strolls towards the elevators. As he walks further and further down the hall, I watch his figure shrink into a scrawny silhouette. From here, his fair skin looks dark, so there really isn't any allure left to him. He's nothing special at all; nothing better than what I know. He's just as familiar to me as the pungent reek of fried hilsa that so often filled my mom's kitchen. He's just as ordinary as the cloyingly sweet jalebis my father would buy every single Eid.

༄

"Where the hell is this fucking bank?" I search the rainy sidewalks for a recognizable street sign.

Imrana and I have been sitting on the bus for almost an hour. We're at the outskirts of the city and still there's no sign of a street called McBride. I wouldn't be so pissed about it if I wasn't so tired and hungry. I haven't had anything to eat since work except for the lollipop I'm sucking on right now.

"Don't worry, she said it would be a long ride," Imrana says, looking relaxed in her seat. "We didn't miss it."

She looks kind of sexy today. She has on her huge looped earrings and has straightened her wavy hair. She's wearing her flashiest clothes and her highest heels. While she'd never go out in public without make-up and stylish clothes, she clearly spent some extra time thinking about her look today. Most girls dress up to impress boyfriends, but Imrana dresses up to impress Sabrina.

The bus driver finds us in his mirror and calls out our stop. There's nobody left in the bus except us. Once we step onto the street, we realize there aren't any people outside either. Sidewalks are emptier when it's raining, but this place is unusually quiet. There are a couple of corner stores open, but everything else is out of business. We stop for a second and take in the scene at the corner of McBride Street. The heavy fog and the darkness of the evening make the neighbourhood seem eerie; everything, from the dilapidated houses to the spindly trees, is shrouded in grey.

"Spooky," Imrana comments as we walk closely together under her umbrella.

"It only looks like this 'cause it's dark," I yell over the noisy rain, maintaining my cool so she doesn't panic.

If I know Imrana and how yellow she is, I know exactly what she's worrying about right now. Serial killers.

"Let's just speed up." Imrana's heels click faster and I try to keep up with her umbrella. "The bank should come right before the second light."

The second light is too far away for a night like tonight. As much as I hate Nelly's Deli, I'm glad I don't have to walk through a haunted neighbourhood to get there. A boring bank job isn't worth this. We're a little jolted when another person finally shares the street with us. It's a boy with his hood and headphones on. Imrana squeezes in closer to me as the harmless kid passes us. Unless she's drunk, Imrana's shy and nervous with almost everybody. The only reason she's normal with Sabrina and me is because we're practically family.

I would like to throw a tantrum when we finally reach the second light and find nothing. All that's here are rows of failed businesses, abandoned houses, and a tall, grey box of a building. There's nothing to indicate what this building is. Its small windows have been boarded up and grated. It's too large to be a house, too small to be a warehouse, and it can't be an apartment building because it has only one floor.

"This must be it." Imrana looks up at the grey block. "Doesn't really look like a bank, though."

"Fuck this, let me just call her." I find my cellphone.

I shouldn't be out here in the rain wasting my time. I should be at home thinking of a scheme to get rich. The one I have pondered over so far is full of problems. Internet scams are a lot more complicated than I thought.

"No, this has to be it. She said it's number forty-three and—look—that's what the sign says." Imrana points to the undersized sign on the building's heavy steel entrance. Under a bold print that reads 666, a fine print clearly says 43 MCBRIDE STREET. "Maybe we should just go in."

"Yeah, I'm sure we'll find tellers inside this dungeon."

My wet shoes and my starving stomach have worn out my patience. I wait for Imrana to open the door and of course she isn't budging. I roll my eyes and grab the handle. "Just follow me."

The heavy door creaks open and I step into a tiny, dimly lit room. Muffled voices and a familiar rap song replace the sound of raindrops. Imrana stumbles behind me and gulps loudly when she sees a monster of a man guarding a wide tinted glass door. His muscular frame nearly covers the width of the doorframe from bicep to bicep. He doesn't scare me much—I've dated guys twice his size.

"Hello, can you help us? We're trying to find our friend, Sabrina Jahan." I have to tilt my neck up to get eye contact with this bulldozer.

He rudely ignores my question and asks us for our IDs instead.

Before I can ask him why, Imrana obediently takes her citizenship card out of her wallet. I take mine out too as I pointlessly try to see what's going on behind the tinted door.

The doorman takes his sweet time to match our faces to our pictures. When he's finally done wasting our time he says, "I don't know any of the ladies by their real names. You can go inside and see if your friend's in there."

Imrana and I look at each other and open the tinted door. Deafening rap music greets us, clouds of smoke, flashes of purple lights —and nipples of all colours and sizes. It's a goddamn strip club.

I turn to Imrana to see if she's fainted yet. To my surprise, her eyes are sparkling with excitement and she's laughing uncontrollably.

"Oh my god!" Imrana covers her gaping mouth. "No fucking way!"

I study the setting like I've never seen it before, but of course I have seen it before in TV crime dramas where the victim is always a nice girl who secretly stripped for her tuition. But standing in the midst of this sexual circus is very different from watching it from afar. These places always look so glamorous on TV because you can't smell the reeking beer, sweat, and tobacco. The seats aren't filled with handsome businessmen or rich college boys, but potbellied drunks with obvious hygiene problems. And the girls? They sure don't look like beautiful TV actresses with perfect bodies, they're emaciated drug addicts with limbs thinner than their dancing poles.

Well, maybe not all the girls. There are three stages on which the strippers do their thing—a large one in the centre and two narrower ones on the sides. On these stand several completely nude, shapeless girls too stoned to dance, surrounded by laughing and cheering hoards, each man with a beer in one hand and a butt cheek in the other.

Nobody's touching the single girl on the large stage though. If you tried to touch her, I'm sure your hand would go right through because she just isn't real. She looks like a plastic doll that some fairy godmother made come alive. She has long golden hair, succulent lips painted bright pink and huge balloonlike breasts. Unlike the limp girls on the smaller stages, she glides her svelte body seductively around her glistening pole. Smiling at the men, she doesn't pick up her money. Their eyes eat her up as money flies around her like unwanted pamphlets on a busy downtown square.

Predatory looks find Imrana and me as we search for the darkest spot in the room. I scan the scene quickly for a brown face. It's become a habit to always check for the presence of a fellow Bangladeshi whenever I'm somewhere I shouldn't be. Although a strip club would weigh equally against them if they told anyone, I'd rather just avoid the awkwardness altogether. If I saw someone from Peckville here, I'd just grab Imrana and make a run for it.

We find an empty table at the furthest corner from the stages and quickly sit down. I don't say anything to Imrana and she doesn't say anything either, but we both look around the place for the same thing: Sabrina.

Imrana searches the brightly lit stages with anticipation, but I keep my eyes on the bar. If Sabrina really works here, then she has to be a waitress or a bartender. I've never had much interest in contemplating people's nature, but I've come to know Sabrina even better than myself. Sabrina may be more colourful than any rainbow, but she'd never make her money by getting naked for ugly drunk guys. I'm sure of it.

"Where is she?" Imrana shouts into my ear.

I shrug and stare impatiently at the bar. I want to see Sabrina come out from behind there with a tray of beers. She can even wear the tiny skirt and netted top that all the other waitresses are wearing. I want to see her laugh at us for believing her bank story. I want to hear her complain about how awful it is to serve drinks to these pigs. I just want her to come out from the bar.

The song ends and so does the gyrating of the human doll. She pouts, evidently not pleased to bend down to collect her money. I don't know why the spoiled bitch is so burdened—if I had a crop that ripe, I'd be happy to spend all day harvesting. When all her bills are gathered finally into a thick stack in her hand, she blows kisses to the hooting crowd. She finds her lingerie somewhere on the floor before she disappears behind a red velvet curtain. Her bare ass is the last we see of her.

A new song begins. There's still no sign of Sabrina at the bar or anywhere else on the floor. There's something about the music that forces me to look at the empty centre stage. The tune is a paradox of sounds: strong exciting drumbeats over a drone of eerie synthesizer chords. And it nearly makes me jump out of my seat. I can feel something bad rushing towards me. Something's coming. Something I'm just not ready for.

Before I can run away and hide, the inevitable happens. The pigs squeal with excitement when a lean, pale leg kicks through the red velvet curtain. They hoot impatiently for their next serving of meat, with shouts of "Come on don't be shy!"

Imrana and I gawk in disbelief because we already know who owns that perfect leg. There's a tattoo of a broken heart on the front of the ankle. It's Sabrina the Heartbreaker.

Sabrina steps onto the stage wearing a tight leather miniskirt and a matching leather bra. For the first time in my life, there's something about her that I don't quite recognize. Her body looks as disciplined as always: it's toned, taut, and limber. Her oversized nose stud, bright baby pink in colour, shimmers in its place. Her long curls are always as dark as evil, and her complexion is as pale as innocence. There's no change in her bony face: she's still more handsome than pretty with her steep nose, strong cheekbones, and narrow jaw. The change, I finally realize, is nowhere on her. It's inside her.

There used to be a power in Sabrina's gait. There used to be a glow of confidence in her sharp, wide eyes. All I see in her now, as she struggles to walk in her seven-inch stilettos, is weakness. There's nothing in her eyes but two black pools of raw apathy. She's been defeated.

Or maybe she's been avenged. Sabrina was always the poorest one of us because her dad died too early and left all the money-making to her mother. She definitely isn't poor anymore as the whirlwind of bills around her proves. Imrana seems a lot happier about this fact than me. Her dimples stay fixed on her beaming face as she watches Sabrina with admiration. She didn't look at me with this much respect when I announced my apartment.

"I can't believe this!" Imrana turns to me and then back to the stage. "She always joked about it, but I never thought she'd have the guts to do it! Wow!"

As Sabrina crawls to the front of the stage, Imrana can no longer contain her excitement. She gets on her feet and joins the drunks in their shameless chanting for Sabrina to take off her clothes. I want to grab Imrana by the arm and force her to sit down, but I can't. If I did that, she'd know just how disgusted I am right now. And I'm not supposed to be disgusted by this. This is cool. This is the stuff that excites us. This is the stuff that pisses our parents off. This is what makes us the free women our mothers aren't and all those good girls from Peckville can't be.

It doesn't take long for Sabrina to spot Imrana's big head in the audience. She waves at us, batting her false eyelashes comically. She tousles her hair and licks her pouty lips. I can't help but smile at her impression of herself as a stripper. Sabrina never does take anything too seriously, but she can't fool me on this.

She's not okay with having her tits and ass on show like inverted rabbits at the window of a Chinese butchery. Our nudity—the shell of our sex—was the one thing we always had complete control over. While our parents and neighbours could watch what we wore, they couldn't watch whom we got naked for. If Sabrina's going to give up this control, then she might as well settle for an arranged marriage and learn how to make samosas.

The crowd is growing impatient because they aren't getting any skin in return for their money. Sabrina has to take off her leather outfit soon. I shout into Imrana's ear, "I don't wanna see her pussy, come with me to the washroom!"

Imrana follows me to the washroom, looking disappointed.

We hang around in the humid washroom for a lot longer than we want to. I sit by the sinks and Imrana leans on a wall as we curiously watch dancers come in and out, gibber to themselves, gibber with each other, or gibber with whomever is on the other line of their cellphones. Because the loud ones are so many, it's easy to notice the quiet ones. The quiet ones don't have the sexy outfits or make-up that the loud ones do. They're young, probably not a year older than me, and intimidated. They will come in with their bloodshot eyes glued to the floor, arms crossed, and shoulders stooped. They'll patiently wait for a free washroom and even yield one to avoid a conflict.

There are a few quiet girls that have been standing around in here almost as long as Imrana and me. They're not doing anything but squinting at the walls and fighting to stay on their platforms. They've had a lot more to drink than their wispy bodies can handle. A few of the other girls have approached them to see how they're doing, but quickly recoiled out of fear that they'll vomit on their shoes or something. I should probably help them to a stall so they can puke out all the poison, but really, there's nothing in it for me. I don't think strippers like to give rewards from their "hard-earned" cash. It's not like any of them would offer to buy my groceries this foodless week.

Sabrina bounces into the washroom, and Imrana and I immediately snap out of our trances. Imrana throws her arms around her and giggles, "You were so sexy up there!"

Sabrina pats Imrana on her back before taking a step back from her. Just like me, Sabrina isn't a fan of being hugged by people—especially not when we're in our bra and underwear. She looks to me and happily accepts a quick smile and a nod.

"So this is what you've been doing for the past two months?" I begin my barrage of questions.

"Six," Sabrina corrects me. "As soon as I turned eighteen."

"Why didn't you tell us?" Imrana asks.

Sabrina doesn't answer, instead she asks me, "Did you get my vodka?"

"Yeah, thanks," I say blankly. But I'm a lot more interested in her answering Imrana's question.

Sabrina changes the topic again. "Imrana, how'd you get out tonight?"

"Library, Daddy."

We all snicker. The library was always our favourite excuse to leave the house.

"All the libraries are gonna close soon—why don't you go and let your parents know that you're coming home?"

Imrana takes Sabrina's hint and wanders away to call her parents. It was never this easy to openly exclude Imrana from a conversation before. We were always a trio of equals. Imrana's no longer an equal and she's definitely aware of it. Sabrina and I have bravely wandered into the forest alone; Imrana's still safe at camp with her scouts.

Sabrina and I stand before each other quietly, each waiting for the other to begin. I never thought I'd ever face a moment when speaking to Sabrina would be so difficult. I've always simply read what was written on my mind and repeated it to her verbatim. But I can't now tell her what I think of her new job. To point out her weakness is to point out my own. To lose status with Sabrina and Imrana is to lose the only status I have in my life.

"You must be loving your new life." Sabrina breaks the tension. "Young, beautiful, and you've got your own place."

I scoff at that. "It really isn't all that great."

"Why? You've got it all."

"I don't even have a TV."

Sabrina doesn't laugh, instead seems to evaluates my issue carefully. "You know, as soon as you told me you're moving out, I knew that money would be a big problem. Money's always a big problem."

"Yeah, tell me about it . . . " I admire the sheen of Sabrina's manicure. "Money's not your problem anymore though."

"No, maybe it's not, but drunken losers, jealous bitches, and horny bosses are." Sabrina waits for my eyes to meet and lock with hers before she finally admits, "The bare-knuckled punches to my pride, Farina—that's my big problem."

I hear her loud and clear. Although I'm desperate for money, I'd never risk hurting my pride over it. For two insignificant brown girls like us, pride is much more important than money. We're born to please our parents, raised to please our neighbours, and married off to please our husbands. Pride is all there is to remind us that we belong to ourselves.

"What can I do to solve your problem, Sabrina?" I surrender to the profound sadness in her eyes. "I'm ready to rob a fucking bank. I just want you out of here."

Sabrina doesn't say it with words, but her smile tells me how grateful she is. Before we both begin sobbing like little girls, she says in her serious tone, "We're not gonna rob a bank. Looking over our shoulders for cops the rest of our lives ain't freedom."

I strongly agree. I really should stop thinking of crazy ways to get rich. "So what do you want to do?"

"Tell me, in this city, who are the richest, most powerful, the most liberated people you see?"

It only takes me a split second to come up with the right answer. The answer is right in front of me five days a week at Nelly's Deli. I say with a smirk, "Fat-cat businessmen, of course."

"Exactly," Sabrina nods. "I've got a car, you talk like a white chick, and Imrana has a lot of time on her hands—we're gonna run our own business."

I'm obviously not the only one with crazy ideas. "What are we gonna sell? We need a product and an actual place to sell that product—we've got neither."

"Wrong. We have both."

"Huh? Where the hell is our store?" I look at Sabrina in complete confusion. She smiles smugly back.

"Your new apartment."

"And what's our product?"

Sabrina looks over her shoulder and directs my eyes to the opposite wall. There's nothing to see there except the wasted young strippers.

"They're our product."

FOUR

"Boys are really smart with their money when they think with their brains." Sabrina lights Imrana's cigarette with one hand and uses the other to take a long drag on her own. "Luckily for us, they think with their dicks a lot more."

We sit in a horseshoe formation in my darkened living room. The only source of light is the narrow strip of sunshine that escapes from between the drawn curtains. Imrana turned all the lights off for some reason. Maybe the darkness reassures her that this "board meeting" is truly secret.

"You never have to worry about the demand in this business. It's been here since the beginning of time and it'll be here until men stop being men." Sabrina's not speaking in her usual sarcastic tone; her smooth voice is forceful and serious. "It's the supply that we have to conquer. We gotta recruit, advertise, organize, provide it—and if we can do that right, we're gonna be rich."

I shake my head to the pack of smokes she holds out towards me. I only smoke when I'm nervy and today I'm calmer than I've been in a long time. The more Sabrina describes her crazy idea, the less crazy it sounds. The more she talks about it so damn confidently, the more convinced I am that I've found a solution to my money problem: the only hurdle to solving all my other problems.

"How rich?" I ask.

Sabrina smiles seductively. "You'll get at least a grand in cash every night. A lot more on Fridays and Saturdays."

My jaw drops, but Imrana's stays clenched. Her legs tremble uncontrollably and her words trip past each other, as she says, "I don't have any doubts that we'll make money. That isn't what I'm worried about. I just know that my parents will find out. I mean, don't we have to do this at night? How am I supposed to stay out all night without them finding out?"

Sabrina and I smirk as beads of sweat make an appearance on Imrana's forehead. She's not doing a good job hiding her lack of courage.

"They will find out that I'm a goddamn pimp. And the first thing they'll do is ship me off to Bangladesh. I'm gonna be forced to work on a farm and smell cow shit all day. I'm gonna marry some ugly fat guy and be pregnant every ten months—"

"Just relax for a second." Sabrina puts a hand on Imrana's knee and Imrana stops shaking. "Your parents will never find out. I've planned it all out. I've thought about everything."

Sabrina puts out her half-finished cigarette and stands up. She hasn't spent too much time on herself today. Her thick curls are collected into a messy ponytail at the top of her head. Her nail polish doesn't match her outfit. There's no make-up on her face except for a few strokes of mascara. She only looks this sloppy when she needs to use her brain. The last time I saw her like this was during test days in junior high. She used to care about school back then.

Sabrina walks up to the window and sticks her head out. I know the view she's so amusedly taking in because it's typical of a weekday midafternoon. It's a demonstration of pathetic integrity. The Aunties and Uncles are marching home from their assembly lines, restaurant sinks, and public washrooms. Dinner is yet to be made. Their kids are hungry for both food and attention. Their families are breaking apart. They don't have a dollar to spend on pretty things. They're tired, disappointed, frustrated. Yet they walk with their heads held high and their smiles stretched wide. They're tumbling through life, and they're proud that, at the end of the day, they're doing it legally.

Losers. It's not their worthless jobs that cripple their attempts at a better existence, it's their worthless morals.

Sabrina stares at the parade of voluntary slaves, her lips curled in disgust. She mutters something to herself before turning to Imrana. "All you'll have to do is the advertising. It's gonna be done online so you don't even have to leave your room."

Imrana's face relaxes, but then she puts on a suspicious frown. "What's the catch?"

"You're gonna make the least money," Sabrina says bluntly. "You're getting a two percent cut; Farina and I are getting forty-nine each."

"That ain't fair!" Imrana pipes up.

"Yes, it is. Farina's gotta pay rent and I've got a mom to take care of," Sabrina hisses. "Besides, we're taking all the headaches and risks; all you're doing is a few hours of uploading every week."

"What headaches and risks?" I stop daydreaming about cash and give Sabrina my undivided attention.

Sabrina bites her lower lip and sighs. "I'll be driving the girls around. If I get stopped by the cops and they realize what's going on, I'm going to jail and never seeing my car again."

"And what about me? What am I doing?" I ask nervously and reach for the pack of smokes now.

"Your English is good so you're gonna be the phone-girl. You're the voice of our agency. You're gonna screen the client, you're gonna find him an appropriate girl, and you're gonna help me set up the appointment."

"That doesn't sound so bad," I shrug. "What's my headache?"

"Well . . . your apartment's gonna be our office, Farina. This is where the girls will wait for their calls, get their make-up ready, and just hang out. This is also where all our meetings will take place."

"Are you out of your mind?" My forty-nine percent share isn't enough to stop my protest. "I don't want a bunch of crazy hookers to know where I live! You know my parents live in the next building; they could knock on the door anytime!"

"You don't have to open it." Sabrina sits down next to me and aims her scorching eyes at mine. She takes a deep breath. "My car, your apartment and our willingness to advertise and set up appointments is our capital. Without these, we've got no business. We've got nothing else to hook the girls. This is not going to work if you can't do that. We don't have the money to rent an office right now. Girls ain't gonna work for us if we can't give them a nice waiting room. They need a safe and secret getaway to do their dirty business all night."

I hesitate to give an answer.

Sabrina presses on, "You're the only one who has a place, do you understand? I only got this brilliant idea after you told me you're moving out. If you don't do this, then our plan and all our money go right down the toilet."

I still don't say anything. The barrage of scary scenarios that play through my mind paralyzes me. One frightens me more than all the others. I imagine a crowd of bottle-blonde, husky-voiced, fishnet-wearing hookers lounging around in my couch. They sniff their coke and chat loudly about their Johns. And then, when I least expect it, my mother batters down my door.

With absolutely no trace of worry in her voice, Sabrina goes on, "If you agree to do this, you'll be able to move out of this shack soon anyway." She looks around the apartment, evaluating every corner. "And when I'm done redecorating, it'll look like an actual office. None of the girls will ever guess that you live here."

Impressed, Imrana unwinds completely and resumes her fawning over Sabrina. "You really have thought about everything."

Sabrina peels her eyes away from me and glues them onto Imrana. "So you're in?"

"Of course I'm in." Imrana sits straight up like a loyal puppy. "But how do I explain the money to my parents? I should get a part-time summer job or something, right?"

"Don't worry about that." Sabrina laughs at Imrana's amateur attempt to connive. "I know people who can put you on a dummy payroll. You'll show a few paycheques to your parents. Get their trust. They'll ask you no questions for the rest of the summer. I guarantee it."

Imrana beams with gratitude. Suddenly, her tone is as strong and fearless as Sabrina's. She looks at me, her upturned nose high in the air, daring me, "Are you in, Farina?"

There's nothing I would love more than to move out of Peck-ville. Having hookers waiting in my apartment is very little to do for a chance at a new life: a dream life with no financial restrictions, no set schedules, and nobody to boss me around. It's indeed very little to do for a chance at complete freedom.

But what if we don't make any money? Maybe it's just my wishful thinking that's so easily accepting of Sabrina's promises. I look at her and Imrana, who both look back at me with opti-mism. They've got nothing to lose. Imrana's got her parents and Sabrina's got her savings. They'll have a roof over their heads no matter what. They don't have to worry about eviction. They don't have to worry about ending up sleeping in a dingy motel bed or a cold park bench.

"I need a guarantee," I demand. "Are you sure this is gonna work?"

Sabrina scoffs at this. "You're the smartest person in this room, so think about it. The city's loaded with businessmen, lawyers, doc-tors, and other important fish. They work too much; their wives don't want them; they've got more money than they can spend. Now, if we come along and offer them young, pretty, fun girls for just a penny of their dollar, don't you think they'll pay? You tell me, Farina, how will this not work?"

I roll my eyes sceptically. "We're only gonna be able to offer scarred-up drug addicts. Who's gonna do this shit if they're young and pretty?"

"Leave the recruiting to me," Sabrina says. "I know who will."

"Who?" I force her to give up every detail.

Sabrina says solemnly, "Everybody."

Suddenly, she looks exactly as she did on the stage. Her eyelids hang heavily over her lifeless eyes. She lets them fall for a long moment. She quietly moans when she opens them to see me, as though she's disappointed that she can't keep them shut forever.

Sabrina gulps loudly and continues. "You remember all those girls in the club?"

Imrana and I nod quietly, still a little shocked by that rare emotional display.

"They weren't all just drug addicts. A few were runaways, some were students, a few even new mothers, and" —Sabrina gestures at her self— "most were just tired of being poor. All kinds of girls become strippers. And I've seen all kinds of strippers become whores."

"How do you know they were fucking the customers?" Imrana takes the words right out of my mouth.

Sabrina hesitates, stares blankly at the floor. Her voice is angry when she's finally able to speak, "The manager encouraged them. Said it'd make them more money and bring him more business. They couldn't do it on his property, of course, so he told them to go out and use the customers' cars."

I shake my head in disgust.

Imrana's reaction doesn't match mine. Her eyes light up and her lips stay parted like she's hungry for more information. She asks eagerly, "Did you ever go to a guy's car?"

"No!"

The deep frown across Sabrina's forehead and the cherry colour of her face reveal just how angry she is at the suggestion. I expect her to fire her mouth at Imrana right about now, but I'm wrong.

Sabrina calms down and says coolly, "Not that there's anything wrong with it, but I never fucked anybody for money. I just didn't want to."

I don't want to ask my next question, but impossible to just ignore it. If I don't ask, I'll have more trouble sleeping tonight. I ask boldly, "If you didn't wanna do it, what makes you think that all those other girls did?"

I think back to Sabrina's angry and miserable face at the club. There was that pain in her eyes that told me she did not want to be there. She wanted me to get her out. And now she wants me to put other girls in. I know I don't win anything by questioning her blatant hypocrisy. There's no profitable reason to pity those faceless girls. A bleeding heart doesn't fatten a wallet. I know better, but logic isn't going to scratch that annoying itch in my conscience.

Sabrina's head jolts back. She didn't expect my response. She regains her composure and explains, "You can't compare me to those other girls. I'm brown."

Imrana giggles. "That's right. White girls are sluts and they like it."

I smirk at Imrana's comment, but Sabrina maintains her composure.

"They're a lot luckier than us. They can do whatever they want with their bodies and they're heroes as long as it's generating money. Who do you see shining on TV? Sexy actresses who can't act and sexy singers who can't sing, that's who," she says. "It ain't about what you are in their world; it's all about what you have. To sleep with a rich man for cash won't ruin them. It's just an innocent business transaction."

My guilt, like a heavy rock in my stomach, begins to feel lighter.

"I'd never push girls to do anything they don't want to do," Sabrina says to me sincerely. "I'm not some sick pimp trying to traffic little girls. I'm not some greedy old man trying to run a brothel. I'm just an entrepreneur who wants to run the best escort agency in this city. I just wanna help those pretty white girls do what they already do."

"And get damn rich off of it!" Imrana cheers.

"Exactly," Sabrina says with a cunning smile before turning to me. "So are you gonna do this or not? Don't be stupid."

I take in the ugly apartment before me. It doesn't look so ugly now that I have to give it up. I say with a bittersweet taste in my mouth, "Yeah."

Imrana hoots happily and Sabrina sighs with relief. They've got what they wanted. I listen quietly as they laugh excitedly about all the things they're going to buy. I won't mention my wish list until the first stacks of bills reach my empty hands.

For now, I got to worry about feeding myself tomorrow.

∽

Her smile is a little skewed. That's the only physical flaw on the woman in the photo before me. She's Eva Merlon, Clint's beautiful wife. I've never met her in person. This picture on Clint's desk is the only piece of information I have on the competition.

As I sit waiting in Clint's office, I wonder if he would ever marry somebody like me. If I was a little older and he was a little younger, maybe I'd have a chance. I'm not white and blue-eyed like his wife, but I'm certainly not as dark as Imrana and my hazel eyes are unusually light for a South Asian. We could always lie to his friends and say that I'm mixed. I could get a nose job and wipe out any hint of my brown ancestry. It wouldn't really better my chances though; Clint knows where I'm from and still finds me attractive.

No, it's not the difference of colour or looks that makes Eva the everlasting wife and me the disposable flirt. It's the obvious difference in our roots. I can just tell by the glow in her eyes that she's never had any problems with money. Her parents were probably just as rich as Clint's. And they probably didn't fight as much as mine did. She was probably never interrogated or yelled at for bringing home anything less than A's. She was probably encouraged to cheerlead, go to summer camp, and travel around the country with her friends. I know her dad loved her and her mom was proud of her because, unlike me, she smiles so effortlessly.

No man like Clint would ever marry the angry girl. They face enough stress at work; all they want at home is something that looks good and talks with no attitude. Girls like me are to them what violent video games are to bored little boys. We're just a temporary escape from their dull, conventional lives. They want nothing more than to play with us for a while.

Clint's heavy footsteps come stomping towards the office, familiar as his cheerful humming. As cocky as he is, he'll probably think that I'm sitting here waiting for him because I want to talk dirty. Not today. Today, I'd like to wave goodbye to my full-time position. I'd like to tell him that I'm no longer spending half my day sweating for him.

"What a lovely surprise." Clint's eyes light up at the sight of me sitting on his chair. "First thing in the morning, too."

I don't bother to return his suggestive smile, and I don't let his freshly shaved face distract me as I announce, "I ain't working five days a week anymore."

"Okay." Clint sighs at his first problem of the day.

He takes off his blazer and reveals a tightly fitted polo shirt. His toned arms, chest, and stomach hover in front of me. I'm tempted. He has a better body than most of the pizza-eating and coffee-chugging boys I met in university. Well, I wouldn't expect anything less from someone who can afford a personal trainer and a private gym.

Clint shuts the door quietly and stands in front of his desk with his arms crossed. "And why aren't you working five days anymore, sweetie?"

I realize that we're completely alone in his office with the door closed. It's seven o'clock in the morning, which means that nobody will come in for half an hour. I have him all to myself for a whole thirty minutes.

With dirty thoughts clouding my head, I somehow manage to

say clearly, "I got a new job."

"You're leaving me?" Clint uses a sad tone I've never heard him use before. I don't know if he's being funny or serious.

He walks up to the little window at the side of his desk and shuts the blinds. The room is dark now. I know what he's doing. I don't know why I'm not stopping him.

"Well, I refuse to let you go."

He must be kidding me. I should be pissed that he isn't taking me seriously, but a part of me is hoping that his words are real.

He comes closer to me and sits down at the corner of his desk. My nostrils fill with his cologne and suddenly I find myself wanting to touch him. It's been so long since I've felt a man. Going to university full time and working six days a week left me too tired to go on the prowl. I was getting used to porn and the feel of my fingers for my boyfriend.

I can go months without the help of a guy, so I know that this urge to touch Clint has very little to do with missing sex. What I really miss is the presence of a male—just that minimal physical presence that I haven't had for almost a month now. I don't miss sex; I miss my dad. Sure, we stopped speaking to each other years ago, but he did breathe and cough beside me. Just to have him in the same room as me, at predictable times of the day, was enough to keep me sane. I know that there are girls out there whose dads simply walk out of their lives like they'd walk out on a bad movie. At least mine stuck around.

I guess what I really miss is feeling I'm somebody worth somebody else's effort.

I play hard-to-get with Clint, although I probably want him right now more than he wants me. I try to ignore the total bliss that overtakes me when his azure eyes target mine. I look away and pretend to be completely uninterested in him. I say without any emotion, "I'll still be here, but only once or twice a week."

I wish I'd never have to see Nelly's Deli again, but I need to be on its payroll for tax purposes. Unless I can point to a legit job, the govern-men will question my apartment sooner or later.

Clint keeps his slight lips closed until I look at him again. "What's your new job?"

"Maid."

"How much are they paying you?"

"None of your business."

Clint chuckles. "You're not being very nice today."

He gets on his feet and comes as close to me as possible. His strong legs touch my knees now. I look up from my chair and take in the beautiful angle of his chiselled face. I've wondered what he'd look like from this viewpoint. It's exactly what I thought it'd be: he looks unconquerable on top of me.

Clint strokes the side of my face and whispers, "How would you like to be my maid?"

The touch of his fingers on my skin is too much for me to bear. I have never had this feeling before. I feel elevated. Clint Merlon, the man with everything, is going to fuck me. I doubted his willingness to go this far before, but it's absolutely certain to me now. The eagerness of his hand and the passion in his voice can't possibly be controlled. He's going to have me, regardless of what he is and regardless of what I am.

"What about your wife?" I find myself asking rather bitterly as I move his hand away from my neck.

"She's not here."

He grabs both my hands and forces me to stand up. He puts his arms around my waist and I nearly gasp. I'm no longer his petty employee; I'm something much more.

Being this close to a rich and powerful man is like being high. I am soaring above a different world right now: a world where I'm not just a crumb on society's collar. I feel his white skin against mine and it's as if his confidence penetrates into my pores. He may not love me, but he's giving himself to me. I am his equal.

"Isn't she good enough?" I probe, testing to see just how badly he wants me. I nod towards his wife's picture. "She's very pretty. Gorgeous, actually. Why do you wanna do this to her?"

Clint says exactly what I want to hear: "Because I want you."

I give him one last test. I escape his arms and shrug, "I'm hardly gonna be here anymore. I don't really need your favours now, do I?"

Clint puts his arms right back around me and whispers into my ear, "I haven't done you any favours yet. Why don't you do this for me and I'll show you what I can do for you."

"What are you willing to do for me?" I whisper back as my fingers relish the hardness of his torso.

He startles me by pinching my nipple painfully through my t-shirt. "For the one day you work down there with those fat cows, I'll pay you for all five days. Is that a good enough price for you?"

I feel threatened by Clint's sudden harshness, but his offer entices me to remain in his grip. Any talk of money trumps whatever else is on my mind or in my heart nowadays. I can't afford to give a shit about anything anymore but cash. I know I'm not going to survive this cruel world without it. I'm hungry. I'm crippled.

"I'm suffering a little bit lately," I confess to Clint. "Would you really do that for me?"

"I'd do a lot more for you. It can't be easy being eighteen and all alone. I'll take care of you."

"How soon can you give me the money?" I ask him readily.

"I can put a little gift in your account today."

"You're lying," I dare him while telling myself that this is too good to be true. It's just too easy.

"I'm a pretty well-off man, Farina." Clint pulls me in closer to him and sniffs my neck while rubbing my thighs. "If I lie, be smart and sue me."

Before I can laugh at his joke, he wraps my hair around his hand and forces my lips to meet his. There's no turning back now. I'm passionately kissing my married thirty-five-year-old boss. This feels wrong. I can never ever tell Sabrina or Imrana about this. Anything I can't tell my best friends has got to be a little wrong.

Clint is not at all the gentleman he pretends to be in front of customers. He only kisses me for a few seconds before he pulls up my t-shirt and aggressively unhooks my bra. He sits down comfortably on his desk and begins to knead my breasts with his forceful hands. I try to kiss him again, but he draws his head back and unzips his designer jeans instead.

"Suck me, you little slut."

I get on my knees and take all of Clint's great girth into my mouth. I don't know how to feel about him calling me what he just called me. If anybody called me something like that on the street, I'd probably take a bat to his head. But it's a whole other mood during sex. This feels normal and familiar. This is intimacy and the only male intimacy I've ever known wasn't very intimate at all.

It's been painful and degrading being invisible to my own father all these years. Being ignored and overlooked like I was nothing. Just a part of the furniture. And maybe now I find comfort in being nothing to whatever male I should be something to. Maybe it's just a quiet reassurance of who and what I am.

No, that's not it. It's probably just nature. After all, they wouldn't have the chick submissive and the dick dominant in almost every porno if it wasn't nature. But what do I know? I'm no psychoanalyst. I'm just a little insignificant Paki girl.

Clint decides that he's had enough of my mouth so he drags me up to my feet by my hair. Suddenly, I don't feel like he's giving himself to me at all. I feel like I've been taken. I feel like I've been stolen.

This is much more than just a business transaction.

FIVE

Most of this May has been rainy and today is no different. Everybody's inside in their warm homes or cars, avoiding the cold drizzle. The only person walking these lonely wet sidewalks is me.

There's a strip mall right outside of Peckville that I have to pass through to get to the bank. There aren't a lot of businesses here: just a convenience store, a hair salon, and a take-out place that serves more grease than grub. Simple supplies for simple people.

When I finally reach the ATM outside the bank, I eagerly get my bankcard out of my wallet. I have to check my balance, see if Clint lied to me or not. After punching in the right buttons, I wait impatiently for the screen to display my balance. It takes its sweet time.

A middle-aged man in a raincoat walks out of the bank. As he stops to open his umbrella, he watches me lustfully. I realize that the white top I'm wearing is completely see-through because of the rain. It clings to my body like Saran Wrap, outlining my shape and making obvious my bra. I watch the man watch me for a long second. I'm surprised to find myself anything but flattered. Actually, I'd like to go up and slap him.

The man smiles amorously at me and continues on his way. My sour mood remains until something else catches my attention: a face in the black of the ATM screen. I hardly recognize my reflection. I don't look pretty, my dripping wet hair is full of tangles, there's no eye shadow on my lids or any gloss on my lips. I haven't combed my hair or put on make-up ever since what happened with Clint. I don't know why.

I stop caring once the screen comes out with the figure. He gave me a thousand dollars.

I can barely feel the raindrops, I'm so stunned with relief. Finally, after so many days and nights of constant worry, a sense of security. Clint has slipped a mattress beneath my fall. I'm going to make it now. I'm going to be fine. You were wrong, Mom. Nothing feels better than proving my mother wrong. So why am I crying?

I need alcohol.

Before I can withdraw some money there's a loud honk behind me. I ignore it but it comes again. I wipe my eyes and cheeks clean of the tears and turn around to see a cheap car with tinted windows.

The passenger window rolls down and there's Ali leaning over from the driver's seat. His boyish smile widens as he sees me recognize him. "Get in!" he screams over the rain.

I don't want Ali to see me with no make-up on, my hair messy, and my eyes red with tears. I don't want to look human to him; I should only be a fantasy. All I want from him anyway is a night or two of fun. I want to steal his glorious innocence like his people stole my freedom. I don't care how beautiful his face is. I won't let him undress me any further than my first layer.

"My clothes are soaked—I don't wanna make your car wet!" I shout back an excuse and turn back to the machine and force myself to stop crying.

"Just get in!" he calls out so loudly that I'm forced to turn back to him. He leans over and opens the passenger door wide.

I give up, rush inside, and shut the door. The noise of traffic and pouring rain is finally muted, but now another unwanted sound invades my ears. A slow duet in Hindi plays quietly from Ali's CD player. The singers' voices are so ridiculously sentimental that I just know the song is about an epic love that surpasses all others. This boy and girl are ready to die for each other.

The last thing I want to be reminded of right now is love—the real kind, that is, not the dinner-then-sex fakery. The real kind isn't for me; it's only for cute, untouched, mentally mint and down-right fake girls. Indeed, fake girls get real love and real girls get no love. Nobody's ever going to love the girl who makes mistakes. Nobody's ever going to love me.

Without taking a single glimpse at my wet shirt, Ali begins to drive. I notice that he's heading towards Peckville so I guess I'll have to get my drinks sometime later. I won't ask him to drop me off at the liquor store. I'm starting to think twice about asking people for favours.

He's staring straight ahead as he asks me, "What the hell are you doing outside in this weather?"

"Just had some business to take care of," I reply, looking away. I really don't want him to see me at my ugliest.

Not surprisingly, there's a hefty pendant with a verse from the Quran hanging from his rear-view mirror. I know that Ali can read Arabic, but I wonder if he has any idea what the words mean. I wonder if he's even a little bit different from his friends, the holier-than-thou hypocrites infesting Peckville and many other ghettos in the Eastside. I hope that all the teachings about compassion, forgiveness, and kindness don't just sit idly on his tongue.

"Is everything okay?" Ali asks, his voice full of concern as we stop at the only light before Peckville.

I scowl at myself in the wing mirror and sigh, "I look like crap today."

"Let me see," Ali commands quickly, tricking me into turning my face towards him. "Your eyes do look a little bit red and tired."

"I don't sleep enough."

"And why's that?"

"I'm worried," I grudgingly admit. "I'm worried about bills and all the other shit you have to worry about when you're on your own. I'm an adult now."

Ali gazes at me with his warm eyes and advises sincerely, "So just be a kid again and go back to your parents."

"I'd rather die." I nod my head with certainty. "I'd rather die than go back to that prison. I'm under a lot of stress, but at least I have my freedom. I can go wherever I want; I can do whatever I want; I can steer my own fucking life instead of just sitting back while my parents run the boat."

"Okay, I guess it's good to steer your own life." Ali rubs his sharp chin in deep thought. "But where exactly is your destination?"

I'm overcome with fear when I realize that I have no answer. I take a deep breath and try to relax. My goal in life is one of two topics that I keep stored away in my mind's attic these days. The other one is of course money, but that's something that shouldn't be a worry anymore according to Sabrina. The issue of what I want in life is something that nobody can help me with—especially not me because I'm pretty clueless. The only goal I can think of is the ability to drink all day and all night . . . until reality becomes as foggy as my dreams.

Hoping that it'll divert Ali from my weakness and frustration, I play with my hair and look at him seductively. However, after a long moment of staring at his face, I find that it's me who's diverted. He sure is good-looking. He could easily be my new favourite distraction, knocking out weed and even vodka.

I flick my upper lip shamelessly with my tongue before I ask him, "Can you come over tonight?"

Ali turns his eyes away and smiles nervously. The light turns green and we begin to move again. The short ride from here to our building is completely silent.

Ali stops at the back of our building and unlocks my door. "You go ahead; I have to go park."

"You didn't answer my question," I pressure him. I might as well pursue what I want from him now that we're talking. I don't have much to lose. My spectacular reputation in this neighbourhood— if I ever had one—is long gone.

"You didn't answer mine," Ali shrugs unapologetically.

"Okay." I feign defeat and say with loud sarcasm, "My destination is some place totally deserted where I can write all day in peace. I want to be a poet. Happy?"

"You're not serious."

I grit my teeth in frustration. "Maybe I don't know what my destination is, okay?"

Ali smirks like he just beat me in a great battle of wits. He writes his cellphone number down on a piece of paper and hands it to me. He declares in a serious tone, "I'm not visiting your apartment any time soon, but let's have dinner some time this week."

I agree enthusiastically—not because I'm dying to date him, but because I'd be a fool to refuse a free dinner.

⌇

The brawny mover greets me with an approving smile. I look down at my lap and pretend like I didn't see him. I can't smile today no matter how hard I try.

Wearing nothing but an undershirt and oversized shorts, I lounge in my sofa with my legs shamelessly spread apart. I have a bottle of whiskey in one hand and a spliff in the other. It doesn't matter which kicks in first as long as one steals my overloaded mind away.

I watch Sabrina direct the mover to where she wants the TV that she just bought. I should be jumping up and down celebrating the return of Mr TV in my life, but I don't find myself excited at all. The reality of what happened with Clint has finally hit me. I can't ignore the sick feeling in my stomach any more. I'm pissed at myself for letting it happen. I'm pissed at him for not stopping himself. What I did was kind of what my soon-to-be employees will do. To be honest, it was exactly the same.

I wonder if this is how sick the girls will feel every night after their shifts. If it is, then Sabrina, Imrana, and I are disgusting for doing this. Girls pimping girls—there's something really disgusting about that. I could and should back out right now, but I need the money. I want the money. Money is freedom on this side of the world, you either milk or get milked.

"What do you think?" Sabrina asks, once the large screen is in place on top of its stand.

I shrug indifferently. "It looks fine."

Sabrina gives the mover a wink instead of a tip and he seems pleased. She closes the door after him and doesn't take a break before turning to me. "All the furniture's coming tomorrow morning. All we gotta do now is go out and get a computer, a microwave, and a coffeemaker. The girls will need a lot of coffee. And so will you."

"Let's go," I say with very little eagerness.

Sabrina waits a few seconds for me to get up. When she realizes that I'm not moving, she takes the whiskey bottle away from me and places it firmly on my table. "Save some for later. We've got work to do now."

I take the bottle right back. "I need this today."

"Why?" she asks. "What's wrong?"

I won't tell Sabrina about Clint, and so I can't name the sick feeling in my stomach, my second thoughts about our little venture. The only solution is to blame our usual suspects for my moral dilemma: our parents.

"What would our moms say?" I ask her. "They'd never look at us the same way if they ever found out."

"Don't do this," Sabrina tells me, "don't go weak on me now. If we want any respect from our girls, we can't show them that we're eighteen and stressing about our mommies. We gotta act a lot older than we are or else they'll think we don't know what we're doing."

"I know that," I reply defensively, "but something about this whole thing doesn't feel right. I'm wondering if it's worth it, you know? We might get a lot of money, but we'll never have a normal life. I'm gonna have to start avoiding my mom. The less I talk to her, the fewer the chances of my tongue slipping."

Sabrina nods her head with understanding, but doesn't sit down for a long discussion on the subject. "You're worried you're gonna miss your parents?"

"Yeah, kinda." I down the whiskey and sulk. "I think they're slowly disappearing out of my life."

"And that's a bad thing?"

Sabrina helps herself to my weed, but not to my alcohol. She never drinks outside of parties. Too many calories.

If Sabrina weren't here, I'd bury my face in my hands and sob like a little girl. I try my best to keep my voice level as I pout, "They made me miserable when they were around, but I'm even more miserable now that I'm alone. I don't think I'm gonna make it on my own. It's so damn hard. It's so damn lonely. I'm fucking miserable, Sabby."

"You're not miserable because of your parents; you're miserable 'cause you've got no money," Sabrina states matter-of-factly. "Parents ain't that important. The only thing they do anyway is steal your free will."

I shake my head with extreme disagreement. "They're my parents. Nobody is more important."

"Why?" Sabrina snaps. "Because they needed some help on the farm and decided to bring you into this joke of a world? You didn't beg and whine to be born."

I guess I somewhat agree with Sabrina, but the alcohol encourages me to argue. "Once you're here, you're here. They've made their mistakes, but they've also been taking care of my back for eighteen years."

"Yeah, and they hate you for that," she says grimly. "They ain't getting a return on their investment. They wish you were a boy. Don't kid yourself."

I don't want to believe what Sabrina's telling me, but what if she's right? Nothing better explains my dad's negligence than a bitter resentment towards me. Maybe he was so pissed about getting a baby girl that he decided to just flat-out deny my existence. Paying for your own essentials is hard enough in this world—the last thing he needed was a puny-armed pussy to feed and clothe. The last thing he needed was me.

I continue to drink my whiskey, every gulp quicker than the one before it. I listen to Sabrina rant, quietly praying that the poison will soon extinguish my burning rage.

"Don't forget that our parents were once just villagers, and daughters mean nothing but poverty and moral trouble in their eyes. If they could turn your tiny body into a tall, muscular working machine, don't think for one second that they wouldn't. If they could trade in your dangerous womb for a portable penis, don't be so gullible and think that they wouldn't. We're useless; nothing but pointless symbols of our daddies' so-called honour. Why do you think they're so hell-bent on controlling our every move?" Sabrina hands me back my weed and stares angrily at the blank walls. "What pisses me off the most is that our moms know all this and still they go along with it."

"No," I immediately refute, "my mom's on my side. I know she loves me."

"Mommy loves me too," Sabrina rolls her dark eyes, "but that doesn't change the fact that she forced me to be a 'good girl' while my dad was still alive. I had to waste my time at the mosque while he went on killing himself with his cigarettes. I'm sure that somewhere in those holy books the prophets wrote that smoking is bad. I'm sure they also wrote that you shouldn't beat your wife or cheat on her. My dad did all that and more anyway. And yet my mom made me pray, five fucking times a day, just to keep him happy. She'd always say, 'Protect your father's name or go sleep outside on the streets where disobedient cunts like you belong."

She takes a deep breath and tries her best to smile like she's fine, but it's more than obvious that she's not. This is the first time she's brought up her dad without the help of alcohol. She can't handle talking about him and all the horrible things he did unless her spirit is on pause. It's just too much to bear.

As usual, I feel completely helpless and weak when I see her depressed about her dad. When the toughest person you know wears her emotions on her face, the problem at hand must be impossible. In Sabrina's case, it really is impossible. She can't confront a corpse. I've always imagined that one day when I'm old and settled, I'd take some time and resolve all the issues I have with my dad. He's still around to keep that wish alive. Poor Sabrina doesn't have that sliver of hope. She's doomed to live with her questions unasked, unheard, unanswered.

I try something I'm not good at: I look at the bright side. Beaming, I tell her, "Your mom doesn't do that anymore, though. She lets you do whatever you want."

"That's absolutely right," she says proudly, "and do you know why she suddenly changed?"

I shake my head, giggling faintly as the weed begins to work its magic.

"'Cause I pay the bigger half of the mortgage payments, that's why. The only way a girl can get some control over herself and her life is when she starts making her own money. She has to earn her freedom. Forget about your parents; focus on your money."

I begin to cackle uncontrollably. Everything Sabrina says sounds so hilarious. I haven't been this stress-free since the last time I was high. Maybe I should be high all the time. I wouldn't complain so much about keeping my feet on this planet if I could just have my brain somewhere else.

"I'm already focused on my money, Sabby." I dumbly gawk at the brilliant shine of her nose stud. "My second thoughts ain't coming from a wish to move back in with my parents and give up my freedom—it's coming from the fact that I see their disappointed faces in my head every time I do something wrong. They've got an invisible leash on me."

"Exactly—" Sabrina gives her approval "—the only leash they have on you is in your mind. It doesn't matter if it's made of love or guilt—whatever it is it doesn't come with an actual chain. You just have to remember that and you'll do alright in this industry. Escape those stupid feelings and there's no limit to how much money you can make."

As I put out the spliff in the ashtray, an interesting thought makes its way to me: "You can't ever run away from love or guilt. They don't come with chains because they can't be attached to you. They're inside you. You'll have to wrench your heart out before you can get rid of them."

"Aw, you were always such a poet." Sabrina laughs and shakes her head at my book collection. "From what I know, poets die locked up in a loony bin with not a single cent in the bank."

"Don't worry, I don't wanna be a poet. I'm just worried about my parents. They're the only family I have. I got nobody else."

"No, you've got me," Sabrina says. It's a promise. "I'm here for you just because I wanna be. I've got no other reason. And that's family."

I smile at my best friend with gratitude.

"We're trying to run a business, Farina. It's time to shrink your heart and grow your brain." Sabrina grabs my hand and helps me up. "Now quit drinking and let's get moving. We're opening in a few weeks. We have shitloads of work to do."

SIX

Three months later . . .

"I'm craving something small and blonde tonight."

I sink into my leather recliner, take a sip of my red wine, and continue to listen to the demands of the pig on the other end of the line.

"Now, when I say 'small', I mean fit. I'm looking for someone very lean."

"All of our ladies are in great physical shape," I boast.

The pig keeps going on and on about how important it is that I don't send him any fat. If he holds up the line any longer, I'm just going to hang up on him. Losing one customer won't exactly leave us in the red, especially not on a humid Friday evening. The city is always hornier when the temperature is high. It's going to be a busy night tonight.

There's nothing I love more than busy nights. Of course the money is a big reason, but it's the hustle that makes me happy. Whereas I used to dread night time, I now long for it. It used to be that empty stretch of time when I was alone with my depressing thoughts, now it's when I lose myself in activity.

Nikki and Jenny giggle as I roll my eyes at the idiot on the phone. Melinda, clearly upset that she hasn't had any calls yet, stares at the TV, her third consecutive cigarette in hand. Africa, the only black girl on our roster, sits calmly on the floor, her lanky legs crossed, reading a tabloid. Like Melinda, she hasn't had any calls today either. But unlike Melinda, she's used to it.

"We have two beautiful blondes available this evening," I happily announce. I can't show any sign of my irritation. The phone girl never gets annoyed, angry or aggressive—she only accommodates. Platinum blonde Nikki and Jenny listen carefully. Brunette Melissa sighs. Africa, with her head full of tight russet braids, quietly continues to read her celebrity magazine.

I turn to the computer on my desk and minimize the window displaying condos for sale. I've been scanning through this website a lot lately. Just another five or six months in this business and I'll have enough money to move out of Peckville for good. Although I'll easily be able to afford a pretty house in the calm suburbs, I plan to get a swanky one-bedroom in the middle of hectic downtown. I have no use for a house. Houses are for big, happy families.

I haven't talked to my mother in months. I only turn on my private cellphone when I need to speak to my sole friend in the real world: Ali. It's better that I just ignore my mother than give her excuses for why she can't come over. If she ever caught a hint of my activities, she'd kill me before I could even stutter out that it's none of her business. Of all the bad things I've done, this is indeed a very special one. Unlike alcohol and sex, this isn't something that all the other kids are doing.

I bring up my spreadsheet for tonight's shift, all the information about the employees in front of me: their appointments, their measurements, their services—and the number of men they'll fuck in a night before the job is no longer fun.

I check tonight's schedule carefully before telling the customer, "I have Jenny who can accompany you immediately and Nikki who will be available two hours from now."

"Which one of them is thinner?"

"Jenny is slightly thinner at five-foot-four, a-hundred-and-ten pounds."

The pig hesitates for a minute before he chuckles, *"Where does most of the hundred-and-ten-pounds go?"*

I cringe as I laugh, "In her perky C-cup breasts."

He hesitates again like this is the most important decision he'll ever make in his life. If he's really that particular about his women, he shouldn't want to fuck a complete stranger in the first place. Just as I'm about to hang up, he finally says, *"Alright, send her over. I'll see her for ten o'clock; one hour."*

"I'll need your name, a traceable phone number, and also the address of where your date will take place. We'll get rid of this information as soon as your session ends."

"I know, honey, I'm not new to this," he says arrogantly. *"My name's Jared Smith. I'm staying at the Northcastle; ask for room twenty-fifteen."*

I write all the information down on a piece of paper and quickly get him off the line with, "Okay, that's perfect. Please be ready with your donation of two-hundred-and-fifty dollars. If you don't call us to cancel before seeing the lady, there is a cancellation fee of forty dollars. Bye, and thanks for choosing the Harem."

"I caught one?" Jenny gets up from the couch and adjusts her low-rise jeans.

"Yeah, but just a warning—" I give her the piece of paper "—he sounds like a real asshole."

"Don't worry; the assholes are always better than the pricks!" Jenny looks to Nikki and they both begin to giggle. They're always drunk and giggling about something.

The incessant noise of girls laughing and chatting was irritating at first, but now I've learned to push it into the background. I'd be naïve to think that they'd ever remain quiet while in here. The tongue always runs quicker when the mind begs to fall asleep. None of them want to remember why they're sitting here in the first place.

Loud or not, I've come to like them. Of our eight employees, there isn't a single one that I have any beef with. I've spent entire nights driving them around, I still don't know their real names, but that's fine because they don't know mine. I don't know about their private lives either, but that's fine too because they don't know about mine. But, ironically, I know their biggest secret and, unfortunately, they mine.

Because I have no choice but to make the girls be my friends, I've let them know that I live here. Sabrina knew most of them when we hired them, and anyone that she can trust, I know I can trust. They're very respectful of my space although they sometimes leave their stuff here by accident. But most important, they know that the bedroom is strictly forbidden. They can have the living room, the washroom, the kitchen, but I need a space that's entirely mine in order to fit all my stuff. I have a lot of stuff nowadays.

It's not too long to ten o'clock so I waste no time and turn my computer off. Just as I'm about to dial Sabrina's number, she calls me: *"'Rina, I'm five minutes away from your place, come downstairs with the girls right now. Oh, and I've got some good news: Imrana's coming out to play with us."* She hangs up before I can say anything.

I'm used to Sabrina's abrupt phone calls. She doesn't mean to be rude; she just hates to have the girls late for their appointments. She says it ruins the Harem's reputation.

"Alright, ladies, let's go." I grab my work cellphone, a pen, and a notepad.

Melinda yawns, stretches, and then finally makes herself get up. She plans to save a fortune from this work and won't let a slow night dispirit her. Nikki and Jenny scuttle to the washroom to fix their hair and make-up. They're always so eager to please their clients—not because they want approval, but because they want tips. Africa looks truly sad as she stays put on the floor. This is the third night that she hasn't earned a single dollar.

She looks up at me with her large brown eyes and says in her mousy voice, "Can I just get dropped home?"

"Are you sure?" I try to be encouraging, "You know it'll get really busy later on. It's not even midnight yet."

"I know, I know, but I'm just really tired. I think I'll just book off."

"Okay, your choice." I cross out Africa's name on my notepad.

I don't really have time to console her as I'm still in my pyjamas. Working all night and sleeping all day has moved my "mornings" to five in the afternoon. I get a little sad when I think about how strange my new life is. When I left my parents, I thought I'd finally be a normal eighteen-year-old. If I was far from it back then, I'm just about completely removed from it right now.

Still, whenever I enter my bedroom with its tall new closet, elegant new vanity and sparkling new mirrors, I realize that I've drifted away in the better direction. Indeed, this is the direction that all normal eighteen-year-olds struggle towards. There is no bigger dream in this world than to be young and rich. The nerds in university don't really give a shit about learning; they only want high marks so they can get high-paying jobs. The ones who pray to God don't pray for world peace; they pray for a winning lottery ticket. I'm already where they all want to be, no school or God needed. They can go ahead and enjoy their normal lives—I'm happy being different as long as the pile of money under my mattress keeps growing.

I open my closet and, as always, break into a smile. My wardrobe is my favourite possession. Designer jeans, shirts, sweaters, jackets, and even socks brim my closet, every piece is expensive enough to both impress and anger the Peckville losers who gawk at them. And, I'm clever when putting an outfit together, the pants not to outshine the top or the top to outshine the shoes. Even if I look tacky, every single piece should equally show out. Let all the Aunties and their perfect daughters see just how many things I own. Let them ogle at what they can never have. Let them be aware that I, the sinner, the dropout, the bad girl, am doing better than all of them.

☙

The warm night breeze caresses my face as I stick my head out the passenger window. Downtown never sleeps on weekends. Roads are loud with traffic; sidewalks bustle with hooting boys and girls; buskers sing and play their guitars, competing with the blaring music from the bars and restaurants. Even hobos are up and awake, shouting out gibberish to snickering passersby.

Like a baby, I take in every sight with wonder. I'm a part of the night scene all the time now, but it still appears new to me. When I was little, my mom had me convinced that people did nothing in this country but work or study. Of course she was lying to protect me from white people and their "sinful" means of entertainment. She thought I'd be fine living in this country and never experiencing its culture. My mother, born and raised in some dairy farm, never did think too deeply.

Sabrina leaves the volume of her speakers way up as she races through the streets. She always keeps her rap music blaring when she's not in the mood to talk to the girls. I know that she's particularly angry at Africa right now.

We're just a few seconds away from Africa's place. She and some older lady share a bungalow in a horribly dilapidated neighbourhood by Chinatown. The lady is a provider herself so she never wonders why Africa always comes home late at night. But I'm sure that it's a great mystery to Africa's seven-year-old twins.

Sabrina stops the car in front of Africa's house and lowers the music. Not turning to look at her, Sabrina says to Africa, "Bye-bye."

"I'll talk to you later," I turn around and smile at the girl as she gets out. "Goodnight."

I watch her as she slowly walks up to her door, tiptoeing like a thief, making sure her heels don't click. Although she's probably dying to talk to her kids, she doesn't want them to wake up and catch her coming in this late. Just like me, she'd rather avoid the people she wants to see than to stand before them looking guilty.

That's really the better thing to do in this business.

Sabrina makes a sharp U-turn, gets back on the main road, and stops abruptly at a light. She turns to me, her black eyes like two hot coals under the red city lights, and warns, "Farina, you gotta let her know she can't just get up and walk out whenever the hell she pleases. For every girl that quits on a busy night, we lose a potential five hundred dollars."

"What do you want me to say? I can't force her to work," I tell her.

"Yeah, that'd be like rape!" Imrana makes a bad joke.

Sabrina calms down and looks thoughtful.

"Besides," I add, "I don't think Africa could bring in that much money even on a good night."

The light turns green and Sabrina begins to race again. She nods at my comment and concludes, "You're totally right. This one is my fault. I shouldn't have hired a black girl."

"But she's hot, though," Imrana contests from the backseat.

"Doesn't matter," Sabrina says, "the only time you could sell a black girl was three hundred years ago."

Imrana begins to laugh hard, but I can only pretend. There's just too much truth to Sabrina's joke for me to laugh. I was pretty sure that racism was dead here until I started this job. Of all our girls, Africa has the roundest ass and the biggest breasts, and yet she's the least popular. Her pretty face and friendly attitude do nothing to increase her business either. Pigs don't call an upscale agency for something they think belongs on the street corner. They don't want to buy dark meat when white meat is available for the same price.

"She won't even take it to the face," Sabrina mumbles. "At least if she did more than the bare minimum, she'd get picked more often."

"Don't get all upset about it," I increase the volume of the music a little in order to relax Sabrina. "It's not like it costs us anything to keep her around."

"Of course it does: it costs us our reputation! We're carrying a brand that nobody wants: it cheapens the entire store!"

I turn to the backseat and exchange a look with Imrana. We're both in awe of this new Sabrina. We've never seen her so serious or passionate about anything. The defeat I saw in her eyes when she was naked on stage at the strip club is never going to return again. She's found something to do.

Before Sabrina can continue her lecture on the importance of a company's reputation, my work cellphone rings. The name on the display brings a huge smile to my face. I giggle and announce to the others, "A 'Shumon Hossain' is calling."

"Uncle wants to get laid tonight!" Imrana laughs.

I shake my head at the faceless Uncle, feeling sorry for the Auntie who I can bet a week's pay he has waiting for him somewhere in the world. I try my best to hide my disgust, speaking into the phone more cheerfully than usual: "Hello, good evening. You've reached the Harem; how may I help you?"

"*Hello? Hi?*" A very nervous Uncle with a strong accent breathes heavily into the phone.

"Can I help you?"

"*Yes, um, I'm looking for girl, um . . .* "

"You've called the right place then. What kind of girl are you looking for?"

"*Do you have South Asian girl?*"

"A South Asian girl? Sorry, not at the moment—"

Sabrina pokes me and whispers, "Tell him we're getting a South Asian tomorrow."

"We are?" I whisper back with surprise.

"We've got an interview with a Mexican. I'm sure she can pass for a brown girl."

I decide not to go along with Sabrina's desperate idea. Even if the Mexican girl looks Indian, there's no guarantee that she'll work with us. There's no point in giving these pigs false hopes—they're already full of them.

I return to Shumon Hossain. "I'm sorry about that, but I'm sure that if you check our website, you'll find somebody that you like."

"*No, thank you, it's okay.*" He quickly hangs up.

"We need a brown chick," Sabrina states.

"We're never gonna find one," I say hopelessly, upset that I've lost yet another customer wanting a South Asian.

Girls from South Asia, and girls from the Middle East and any other soil that Islam has dug its talons into, are as rare as diamonds in this city's sex industry. I don't think I need to explain why.

"Do you have any idea how many e-mails I get from rich white regulars wanting South Asian girls?" Sabrina's eyes widen with ambition as she declares, "We'll fly into the slums of Dhaka and bring one over if we need to. We're finding a brown escort by the end of this month no matter what."

"I can't believe brown girls are so wanted," Imrana says proudly. "I know desperate Uncles want us, but white guys are calling too? I thought they found us ugly."

"They did," Sabrina smirks. "Until we started shaving."

"And exercising," I add.

"And working in their offices . . . " Sabrina continues.

"Being their secretaries," I continue.

"Their cute weather girls . . ."

"Their sexy nurses."

"And then there's Bollywood . . . "

"Where all the girls are perfect."

"No, we ain't all hairy and ugly anymore."

"We're 'exotic'."

Sabrina and I look at each other with surprise. She's contemplated this issue as much as I have. Maybe it's because, unlike Imrana, we're used to white guys checking us out.

"Well, I hope the Mexican passes." Imrana suddenly thrusts forward so that her head is between Sabrina's seat and mine. "Let's go to a bar!"

"A bar? We're in the middle of work!" Sabrina exclaims.

"Come on, I never get to stay out all night with you guys. Let's just close shop and go party instead."

"We don't 'close shop' to go party. This is a legit business and a legit business is open for all the hours it says it's open," Sabrina says. "But since you're here tonight, we'll grab a few cocktails after I pick up Kelly and Bambi."

We turn into the Westcastle Hotel's driveway, where we get stuck behind a line of taxis, limousines, and other expensive cars. Sabrina's jet-black BMW blends right in.

A statuesque blonde in a belly-baring top stands outside the entrance. Only Bambi, our most popular employee, would dare to wear an outfit like that to a fancy hotel. I wave her over and she smiles brightly when she sees me. She swings her hips and struts towards the car as the valets gawk at her with lust.

Bambi isn't particularly pretty, with her crooked teeth and comical close-set eyes, but her overall look seems to excite any man she walks by. Her melon-sized breast implants are ridiculously disproportionate to her spindly body. Her bleached hair, stuffed with extensions, resembles a lion's mane. Her revealing clothes are pressed with glitter, or embroidered with beads, or lined with faux fur. She's our most wanted girl because she's exactly what customers seek: an escape from reality. They forget that she's just regular skin and flesh behind all the dazzling make-up and sparkling jewellery. They don't pay for Bambi—they pay for a toy; a magic trick; a psychedelic experience.

Bambi gets into the car, greets us in her husky voice, and laughs, "That was, like, the most amazing guy I have ever had."

Sabrina feigns interest as she speeds out of the driveway. "Really? Why's that?"

We always feign interest in whatever stupid thing Bambi has to say. The top employee must be treated like a queen. If we lose her, we lose a lot of money.

Bambi touches up her make-up. "He owns a resort in one of those sunny islands, you know? And he told me he could get me a room for free! Like, completely free for me and a friend—anytime of the year that I want!"

I scoff, "Are you sure he didn't want to be that friend?"

"No, he said to bring one of my girlfriends! All I have to do is give him a call a few weeks before my trip," Bambi replies.

"I'm happy for you," Sabrina rolls her eyes. "Your next call is just a few minutes away, I'm just gonna get Kelly first."

Bambi groans loudly. "Can't you drop me off first? I don't want be in the same car as that bitch."

Bambi and Kelly can't stand each other. When Bambi's regulars get bored with her they always switch to Kelly, and vice versa. It shouldn't be a huge deal—after all, the girls know that none of the clients sign up for a long-term relationship—but it clearly bothers them. It can't be easy to find out you're no longer desireable to a client.

"We ain't got time for a round-trip." Sabrina pulls into the ritzy neighbourhood where Kelly's just finished a call.

The girl comes walking down the sidewalk when Sabrina stops the car and honks. Our second most popular employee, Kelly is a gorgeous brunette that Sabrina used to dance with. The first time I saw her, I wondered how a girl like her possibly got into this business. With looks like hers, she could have had a great future in the trophy-wife department. But I guess being a trophy wife isn't that much better. At least hookers are free to leave in the morning.

Kelly exchanges a happy smile with Sabrina, Imrana, and me and grudgingly sits in the back with her rival. The girls always look the happiest when they return to the car from a completed call. It's probably because they got themselves and their money safely away from the infinite number of dangers possible in a room with a naked stranger. I doubt it's ever because the sex was good.

Kelly asks what's happening tonight and Sabrina lets her know that we're going drinking. As soon as Kelly invites herself, Bambi complains that she's not feeling very well. Kelly goes on endlesslyabout a new bar where all the yuppie snobs like to party, where martinis cost fifteen dollars. Imrana sighs loud enough for Sabrina and me to take note. Unlike everybody else in the car, she doesn't make enough for fancy drinks.

Sabrina looks at the rear-view mirror at Imrana and says, "Your drinks are on me tonight."

"I'll get you a few too," I say needlessly.

Imrana happily accepts our offer with an endearing display of her dimples. She looks just as exhilarated as I did that first night I rode with Sabrina. I pity her for choosing to get a diploma over doing this job full time. This is a much better life for people like us. This nocturnal wonderland lifts all those weights that crush us in that other world. Here, boredom doesn't exist, anonymity strengthens presence, and achievement is possible with every ring of the telephone. No silly piece of stamped paper is going to hand all that to a moneyless brown female with no family, no community, no social lifelines of any type. Imrana will learn that when she grows up.

Sabrina orders everyone to shut up as my cellphone rings. I answer with my usual enthusiasm.

Sabrina swerves into a neighbourhood where the houses are so tall they dwarf the trees. She stops the car and unlocks Bambi's door. Careful not to disturb me, Sabrina gives Bambi a quiet thumbs-up after passing her a tiny plastic bag full of pills. The Employees hate receiving these bags because it means that their client is old. Older pigs will often buy a pill to help them stay hard longer even though they know that we overcharge by a good thirty dollars. I guess you can't put a price on ego.

Holding her purse tightly Bambi walks up to the two-storey

house across the street. With its neatly trimmed hedgerow and vast garden full of pretty flowers, you'd think the owner was the law-abiding type. We watch as Bambi knocks on the door. A portly man, his shirt unbuttoned, opens up. Even though we're parked a good distance away, we can see the thick curls on his spotty chest. His flushed face is wrinkly and the few strands of hair left on his head are completely grey. He must be at least twice Bambi's age.

Yes, I feel sorry for her, but it's just for an hour. It's just one hour of her life. All she has to do is grin and bear it for sixty minutes and she's free to walk away with two-hundred-and-fifty dollars. Yes, we'll be taking close to half that amount, but she's still getting one-hundred-and-forty. What other job pays a-hundred-fucking-forty dollars per hour? My mother would have to break her back for two days at the factory to make that amount. Bambi's the winner in this game. Women are the winners in this game. I remind myself that I have no reason to feel guilty as I watch Bambi disappear into the house.

As soon as the door shuts, Sabrina drives away and I give the pig on the phone my undivided attention. The night goes on.

SEVEN

Morning brightness forces my eyes open. I begin to lift my head to see where I am, but a sharp pain in my neck forces me back down. A large cockroach crawling on the white ceiling is a hint that I'm in my apartment.

"About time you woke up," Sabrina says, leaning over me. From my angle, she looks ten feet tall and more than able to crush me with a single stomp of her foot. "Hurry up, we've got an interview to do."

"God," I groan. I'm way too hung-over to get up now. "What time is it?"

"Eleven-thirty. We have to meet the Mexican girl at noon." Sabrina already has her shoes on.

I realize that my neck hurts because I've been using Imrana's meaty thigh as a pillow. She's sleeping next to me on the floor of my living room. Her jeans lie low at her waist and her perky little tits are exposed. I yawn and push her dark brown nipples back into her bra. I check out her shirtless body before I drag myself up. Her stomach is quite flat for someone who has soda for breakfast and gummy bears for dinner. It's not as lean as mine or as sculpted as Sabrina's, but it's still quite nice, I must admit.

Sabrina hands me a cup of coffee before she bends down to force Imrana awake. I quickly put the coffee down on the table and sprint to the washroom. All that overpriced bar food I forced down last night is definitely coming back up.

I drop to my knees and hunch over the toilet, moaning with pain. My nostrils fill with the filthy smell of the soiled toilet seat.

This is the duller facet of my bejewelled new life.

As my tired eyes hover over the stained bowl, I become aware of the mundane sounds of the world out there. I never before paid attention to the chirping of birds; the tinkling melody of the ice cream truck; the idle prattle from the neighbours. These sounds come from outside my window, so close. But I'll never feel part of them again. I have too many secrets. Now that the numbing effect of the alcohol has worn off, I feel a surge of something that must be loneliness, and I wish that I didn't have to face a single minute of the rest of my life sober.

"Are you gonna be fine?" Sabrina shouts from the living room.

I violently throw up into the toilet. My throat burns as I shout back, "No!"

Sabrina comes marching in. She helps me get up and directs me to the sink. I'm surprised that she sounds more worried than annoyed. "I told you to go easy on the drinks."

She holds my hair as I bend at the sink to rinse my mouth and wash my face. I stand up straight for a few seconds and then another roll of my stomach forces me back down.

"Wash your mouth out again," Sabrina instructs me gently.

As I'm washing my mouth, I feel Sabrina's hand find my forehead. She douses her hand in cold water, then returns it to cool me. Her hand stays still at first, but then very slowly her stationary touch graduates into a gentle stroking motion. Sabrina comforts me lovingly, with the same soothing hand my mother placed on my forehead all those times I suffered a fever as a kid. It's protective, possessive, but most obviously it's caring.

I realize how much I miss having someone take care of me. As soon as I hit thirteen, I told my mother that I could take care of myself. I was so certain that taking care of me was just another way for her to control me. I would be irritated if she asked me how I was feeling, furious if she ever brought me medicine. But no matter how angry I got, she never stopped. I knew she'd never stop.

I'm probably imagining that Sabrina's gesture is out of more than simple worry for a sick friend. I simply wish that her hands were my mother's. All I can think about when I'm sober is my mother. I miss her.

There's nothing left in my stomach so I stand up straight without fear of vomiting again. I give Sabrina a sincere smile and say, "Thanks."

Without emotion she replies, "I just want you to be good for the interview."

There's no way I'm going out to do an interview now. I was surrounded by employees all yesterday and talked to strangers for sixteen hours; I deserve a little sleep and a few moments to myself. Not everybody can be as energetic as Sabrina. I towel my face dry and raise my voice a little. "Just see the girl without me. You're a better judge than I am, anyway."

Sabrina raises her sharp eyebrows. "I've told you before that I don't like doing interviews without you. This is your company as much as mine. Don't you want to know who's working for you?"

"Of course I do," I point at my sunken face, "but I'm fucking dying here."

I can tell that she's not pleased, but she knows she can't say anything to change my mind. We're equally stubborn.

"Plus, I gotta be fresh for tonight. It's Saturday, the phones are gonna ring nonstop." And I regretfully remind myself, "And I have to get my ass to the deli tomorrow at eight in the morning. Sorry, but I need sleep."

Before Sabrina can recommend coffee, we hear Imrana's drowsy voice calling from the living room: "I'll go with you, Sabby!"

We leave the washroom to find Imrana, still in her bra, smiling at us from the couch. Her lipstick is smeared all over her face and her hair sits like a bird's nest on top of her head.

"Don't you gotta go home?" Sabrina asks curiously.

"Yeah, how long did you tell your parents you're staying over at

Hasina's?" I join in, more worried than curious.

Hasina's one of Imrana's nerdy acquaintances from high school. She's the only girl Imrana is allowed to have sleepovers with. Her parents don't trust me, her friend of nearly twelve years, but they're fine with Hasina. I guess you're automatically an angel when your dad's an imam.

Imrana stares at us, her lips tightly pressed together. She looks down at her bare belly and says quietly, "I didn't tell them I'm going to a sleepover."

Sabrina and I give Imrana a puzzled look and say in unison, "What?"

"I ran away. I'm not going back home."

I look at Sabrina, who makes a gesture of despair and casually takes a seat, dismissing herself from the unfolding drama. I wish I could take this lightly too, but I can't. I'd be the hypocrite of the year if I told Imrana to get her ass back home. I kind of ran away too. On the one hand, I am free now. On the other hand, Imrana's not me. Imrana's not ready to make it on her own. Her skin isn't tough enough and the gears in her head need oiling. She's a kid. She's a child. Children need their parents more than they need freedom.

After some thinking, I sit next to Imrana and look directly into her round eyes. "You need to get your ass back home."

Imrana snaps at me, "You, out of all people, are telling me to go home?"

"Both of you relax." Sabrina stops the fight early and comes to sit in between Imrana and me. "Why don't you tell us what happened?"

Imrana crosses her arms, takes a deep breath, and talks to her feet, "I got yelled at pretty bad yesterday."

"What did you do?"

"I was talking to a guy online. Nothing special, I was just bored. I asked to see his face so he sent me a pic." Imrana gulps loudly. "I open the file and there's a lot more than just his face. His dick is all over my screen and my mom's watching it from behind me."

"Damn." I bury my face in my palms, pointlessly trying to escape the perpetual and ever-growing stress of my life.

Sabrina is perfectly calm as she asks, "What did your mother say?"

"The same old. She told me that I have no morals, that I'm a dirty girl, and that not even God can fix me." A wry smile forms on Imrana's lips. "She called me a 'whore' and that's when I got up and left."

Sabrina puts her arm around Imrana and nods pensively to herself. "You did the right thing."

I look up at Sabrina with surprise. I can't believe she thinks that this is the right thing for Imrana. I quickly interrupt their triumphant moment: "Where the hell do you plan on living?"

"Here?" Imrana shrugs.

"Here? You're gonna catch your parents in the elevator every day. Believe me; they'll drag you home by the ponytail. You can't stay here." I look at Sabrina—if I can persuade her, Imrana will surely follow.

"It'll be for a very short time," Imrana says, more to convince herself. "I'll start looking for a condo tomorrow."

I try to catch Sabrina's eye so I can hint that I need help, but Sabrina keeps her indifferent gaze on her fingernails. I yell at Imrana, "How the hell are you going to afford a condo? You make a hundred illegal dollars a week—no bank is gonna give you a loan!"

"Well . . . about that," Imrana hesitates, "I was thinking I work with you guys fulltime and we can split the money equally. I'll work a regular job on the side, just like you do, Farina."

Sabrina suddenly wakes up. "We'll discuss this later. We're running late for the interview, we should get going now."

Imrana springs up and, in an excited attempt to show Sabrina her passion for the job, she heads straight towards the door. I stop her just before she puts her hand on the knob: "You might wanna put on a shirt."

Imrana blushes. "I think I left my top at the bar. Do you care if I grab something from your closet, roommate?"

I roll my eyes and kiss goodbye to my bedroom, the only private place I had left. "Go ahead. Take whatever you need."

Imrana disappears into my bedroom and I'm left alone with Sabrina. I say in a low voice, "You know her parents will be coming here to look for her, right? What the hell will I say?"

"You'll say that she's our worry now," Sabrina mumbles, as she clicks away on her cellphone. "I'm calculating your cuts."

"Why? There's no hurry."

"I just wanna get it done with," she insists and takes out a bulky envelope from her purse. She calls to Imrana, "Come get your money!"

Imrana comes out smiling from ear to ear, wearing one of my favourite t-shirts. She never needed cash as much as she does now.

Sabrina takes a thick stack of bills out of the envelope and holds it in front of us. She proudly announces, "We had thirty-one calls yesterday. We made a total of three-thousand-four-hundred-and-ten dollars."

Imrana and I clap and cheer for a very good night. Sabrina sorts the money on the living room table before handing Imrana a rather thin pile. "Here's seventy bucks for you."

"Thanks!" Imrana holds her money tight and feels the texture of power, distinction, survival, and freedom. She giggles with pure joy.

But her giggles fade fast. She sees the wad of bills that Sabrina gives to me.

Sabrina makes no effort to divert attention from our cuts. She never really was very good at sparing people's feelings. "Here's one-thousand-six-hundred-and-seventy for you," she happily lets me know.

Imrana doesn't make a peep of discontent. She puts her share in her purse and eagerly heads for the door. She pretends like she didn't notice how much money Sabrina and I got, but I saw her stare at me when Sabrina gave me my share. I saw her gawk at the bills in our hands with a thirst I know only too well.

&

I scratch my ankles uncontrollably as I tread up the steep hill. The mosquitoes are having a feast on my tender skin. I wanted Ali to come to my place so that I could finally take what I want from him, but he insisted that we come here to the city's biggest park instead. I've been so desperate to spend some time with him that I agreed without too many complaints. So here I am, spending my last few hours before work sweating in the scorching heat, being bitten by insects and ruining my designer shoes.

"Nobody ever comes here," Ali says as he grabs my hand and helps me up. "Too lazy to walk this far."

I've been to this park a hundred times before to smoke with Sabrina, but I've never made the long walk to this secluded area. This hill is a great distance away from the beach, where all the happy people of the world frolick under the sun. Although my legs are exhausted from the journey, I don't really find myself resentful at all. I'm honestly pleased to be here all alone with Ali in the pure calm of nature. This is the perfect escape from the carnival that has become my life.

When we finally reach the top of the hill, we gape in awe at the panorama before us. From here, the quiet teal lake seems to never end. The shoreline, dotted with the matte grey of rocks and the subdued green of shrubs, is as calming to the eyes as the summer breeze is to the skin. Geese glide gently close to the shore or wobble on the rocks, making no sound except the occasional honk. It's the people out there who destroy the peace with noise from their speeding boats. I try to focus on the horizon, where the beautiful lake and the lonely sky kiss, but my eyes are drawn to the speeding boats. I could so easily afford one of them. I too could own a boat.

We catch our breaths and sit down on an old bench nearby. Ali gazes upon the lake contentedly, not noticing me looking at him. As I gaze up at his strong profile, I wonder how much longer I have to wait for him to visit my apartment. I wish he'd just give it up already and take all my stress and tension away. My nights would be so much easier if I could have him over during the days. We could just get high and make love for hours. We could leave the world and all its problems behind. We could be a normal couple.

We're far from a normal couple. Nobody knows about us except for his crack-head friends who always need him for a ride. I'll tell Sabrina and Imrana eventually, but I know that they won't be happy when I do. They won't think of Ali as Ali; they'll just write him off as another poor Bangladeshi from the holier-than-thou club. And those are the type of guys that we've always hated. They're our dads in progress: they all grow up to be selfish and self-righteous chauvinists who treat their wives like servants and their daughters like inanimate possessions. I'm definitely not going to be congratulated on my choice.

I think about the ridiculous lengths that Ali and I go to in order to hide our so-called relationship from the nosy Aunties. I couldn't care less about those neighbourhood "reporters," but Ali has his pristine image to uphold. If we're ever in the same elevator and some Aunties or Uncles are there, we have to pretend like we don't know each other. When we use his car, I have to walk a block away from Peckville so that nobody sees him picking me up. Pathetic.

I know that this is what I signed up for when I decided to chase a good boy from the motherland, but I was ready to do the extra work in exchange for his tall, hard body. I thought that he'd come over regularly and satisfy both our needs, but it's been almost three months now and he hasn't touched me. He hasn't even kissed my lips.

"We're totally alone here," I say suggestively as I rub the back of his neck with my fingers. "We can do anything you want."

"Anything I want?" Ali looks at me lustfully.

"Anything you want," I tempt him.

"Alright—" he gently moves my hand away from his neck and peers into my eyes "—I wanna talk."

I sigh loudly to mark my disappointment and increasing impatience. I move away from him slightly and again I contemplate our relationship. I seriously debate whether he's worth my time and my fidelity. Sure, he's sexy, but that doesn't really matter if I get no sex from him. He's got no money—even if he did, I know that I've got more. He's no good for parties: he doesn't drink or smoke. It's quite clear that I don't need him; the mystery lies in my total inability to be rid of him.

I sit back as far as I can on the bench and take out a mini-sized bottle of vodka from my purse. Ali scoots closer to me and slides an arm over my shoulders. He gently takes the bottle away from me and shoves it back into my purse. "Don't do that to yourself," he orders me with genuine concern, and suddenly I realize why I do actually need him.

I need Ali to respect me and I need him to be my friend. I need him to prove to me that guys still care about girls: that there exist outside my crazy world guys who could never so easily separate a girl from her sex, buy one and expect the other to follow. I need Ali to sustain my hope in men. I don't want one day to believe that they're all monsters.

"I like your outfit today." Ali swiftly checks out my top and my jeans before he stops suspiciously at my sneakers. "You can't get those cheap. Did you get a raise at the deli or something?"

"No, I just took up another job with a catering company. It's good money during summer, you know, with so many weddings happening and shit," I lie without blinking twice.

Lying is no challenge for me these days. I lie to pigs all the time about how perfect my employees look. I lie to my employees all the time about how much Sabrina, Imrana, and I care about them. I lie to everybody at Nelly's Deli about what I do on my days off. I lie to my mother. I lie to the bank. I lie to the police. I lie to the govern-men. Lying has become more normal to me than telling the truth. Its tell-tale twitches can't be found on my face anymore. But they do continue to jolt me somewhere in my chest.

"I know you've been working hard. You look tired."

"I am tired." I wish I could confess to Ali about that other world. "I am really tired."

"It's not too late to go back to university and fix everything." Ali's deep voice is firm but also sympathetic. "Get a degree if you want freedom so bad. Go back to your parents' and let them worry about the rent while you make a future for yourself, Farina. Two dead-end jobs might as well be slavery. What were you thinking, dropping out?"

"I hated university," I state shortly.

"Why?"

"Because I couldn't fit in there just like I can't fit in anywhere else. All the teachers in high school said that 'university will help you find yourself', but I felt as lost and lonely as I always have," I admit very frankly. "I remember my first ever tutorial; it was for European History, I think. I walked into the classroom with my fake fur jacket, my chunkiest earrings, my no-name jeans and my five-inch boots. I was one of just three girls in a class of, like, fifteen and obviously the only brown person in sight. I had 'ghetto' written all over me and even though nobody said anything, they were sure thinking something."

"I hear you," Ali nods with understanding, "you gotta pretend to be somebody you ain't if you wanna be taken seriously on campus. You gotta imitate the people here."

"I just don't belong in that boring place. I'm never going back."

"Are you a hundred percent sure about that?"

I twist towards him so that he's forced to see the implacable expression on my face. "Yes."

I can see the still lake in Ali's brooding eyes. I can tell by his silence and his deep breath that he's worried about me. I know that the right thing to do is to reassure him that I'll be fine, but I stay quiet because I'm far too much in love with this rare moment. Somebody other than my mother is actually worried about me. A boy is worried about me.

After a long moment of thought, Ali shoots, "Look, Farina, the white man's world ain't fair, but if you work within his system and really use your head, you win the game."

"No, I don't win the game. I lose if I waste my youth reading books I don't wanna read just so that I can get a job I don't even want." I sigh and open up to him completely: "I'm sick and tired of being controlled, Ali. Reality is that I'm a girl and I live in Peckville, which is the same as living life with my head held underwater. I'm fuckin' suffocating! All I want is to get out of there. I don't wanna waste my time trying to be a goddamn doctor or lawyer, I just wanna be free."

Ali chuckles and asks, "You really think that Peckville is the only place out to control you? Unless you put up a tent in your own little jungle, most aspects of your life are always controlled by people—by society. The only thing you've got absolute control over is whether you wanna listen to your conscience or not. Nobody can force you to ignore God's instructions. To do what feels right is to practice the only real power you have."

If Ali's right, then I guess I've got no power. I've muffled that nagging voice inside me so many nights now that it's become nothing but a faint whisper. When I'm hustling in that other world, dreaming about my downtown condo, money always talks the loudest.

" . . . And that's why I wanna be a doctor," Ali declares self-assuredly.

I shake my head with restrained disgust. "Are you sure it's not because your parents told you to? I mean, that's like every brown parent's dream— being in the west with a kid who's a doctor."

"I can't argue with that," Ali laughs. "I've been told my whole life that all other careers are trash. My dad would kill me if I decided to do something else. My mom would probably disown me."

"That sounds like textbook brown parenting," I mutter.

"Yes, but I really want to be a doctor." Ali looks up and stares searchingly at the sky. "I have to become a doctor if I wanna do what my conscience is telling me to do."

"And what's that?"

"I have to go back to Bangladesh. I have to go back and do something—build a proper hospital in my village; set up free clinics in the slums; do a country-wide tour explaining hygiene—I don't know what, but I have to do something. That's my dream."

"That's a beautiful dream." I watch Ali's distressed face with admiration, clutching his hand tightly.

"We betrayed our country once when we decided to leave all the chaos behind for burgers and malls. We'll betray them twice if we never go back." Ali taps his foot anxiously. "I ain't gonna die happy unless I know that I tried to help."

"Why do you care so much?" I ask.

"I've got an image stuck in my head, Farina." Ali slides down and rests his head on my shoulder, taking a deep breath before he begins, "It's of this teenage boy I saw when we visited Dhaka two years ago. He was sitting on the street corner begging for food. He was completely blind. We were stuck in traffic so I watched him for a long time from the car we had rented. I saw so many people walking by, kicking his arms away when he grabbed their ankles, just begging and crying for something to eat. Then this group of guys come and finally hand him something. He puts it in his mouth and spits it right out, cursing at the guys, who just laugh at him like he's a clown. What they gave him was cow manure. He couldn't protect himself because he couldn't see. He'll never be able to protect himself 'cause nobody's ever gonna buy him a surgery. That boy's gonna beg and be humiliated for the rest of his life. Nobody in the world gives a damn that he's blind."

I kiss Ali's forehead in a pointless attempt to comfort him. I cross my right leg over my left knee and suddenly the tip of one shoe becomes visible. The vinyl toe shines so brightly under the sunlight that it hurts my eyes. I quickly put my leg down and tuck my feet under the bench, gulping heavily as I watch the priceless horizon.

"I'm willing to pretend to be somebody I ain't if it'll help me make my dream come true. I choose to listen to my conscience. I'm gonna do what feels right. That's my idea of freedom."

EIGHT

"Oh, we were so in love," says Ben, dreamily reminiscing about his ex-wife. "In college, we'd skip our lectures almost every day just so we could sit under the trees and talk about nothing."

Ever since I started spending my shifts lounging in the lunch-room, I've become the old caretaker's friend. I'm such a good listener that he's always eager to tell me all the most private and interesting details of his life. His stories aren't half-bad, and it helps me that he's never out of them. The longer he chats with me, the shorter my pointless shift at Nelly's Deli seems.

"That's probably why neither of us graduated!" Ben looks up and grins.

I chuckle, reminded of how I also quit university, and slowly sip my coffee. "So why did she leave you?"

Ben looks down at his wrinkled hands. "I don't think she was ever really in love with me. When we met, she was already on the search for love. She had her love story written out and I fitted the part of her imaginary prince. She forced herself, no matter how unhappy she was, to forgive all the little mistakes I did. She changed herself to please me and I really thought that our relationship was perfect. She realized after ten years how impossible it is for a woman to live with her pride in her throat, so she spent the next five years of our marriage trying to change me. When she found out that I was incorrigible, she gave me the papers without a second thought."

"Sorry to hear that."

"My life went down the hill after that. I never got another lady because I lost my looks along with my charm. I was forty years old, but I drank so much that I looked years older. The drinking took my job, my health, my kids." Ben's voice breaks. "I hardly saw my babies after she got custody. If there's one piece of advice I can give you, young lady, it is to stay far away from the Devil's nectar. The juice tricks you into believing that it's fixing your shattered life when it's really only crushing its shards."

"Maybe you're right," I shrug, knowing quite well that he has a point. "Your kids . . . they must be grown up by now. Do you see them?"

"My ex-wife didn't wait too long to find them a new daddy. They forgot all about me. I call them every week to hear their voices, but they always have an excuse to cut our conversations short. One's a nurse and the other's a teacher; they don't have much reason to talk to an old drunk like me."

I stare at the sadness and longing in Ben's watery eyes. I have not once seen this kind of love in the impenetrable eyes of my father. He hasn't called once since I left. I look at Ben with admiration. "You may like the bottle a lot, but you know what? You're a good dad," I tell him.

"Yes, I may have been a lousy husband, but I have always been a good dad," Ben says proudly. "I'll be a good dad until my babies bury my bloated body. Remember me as that poor janitor who loved his children until his very last breath."

"You won't be a janitor forever, Ben," I try to cheer up the old man. "This wonderful country has a pension plan for old people."

Ben laughs. "Oh, you young people! You're so used to money falling from the ceiling of your parents' house that you think the skies rain money too. A pension only pays for one meal a day and I'm a hungry man. Money never comes easy, sweetheart."

"I disagree," I say with a sure grin, picturing the tens of thousands of dollars under my mattress.

"You'll agree soon enough, pretty young girl," Ben says with an equally confident smile, sticking his fork into his lunch of over-cooked pasta and defrosted peas.

The door flings open and Olga, the craziest one of the hags, screams at me, "What are you doing up here? Where's your hair-net?"

"I'm on my lunch," I say without acknowledging her. "And I already told you that I'm not wearing that ugly thing anymore."

"Your lunch ended half an hour ago!" Her double chin wobbles with every loud word.

"Fine, I'll be down in a few minutes." I turn my face away and mutter, "You fat-ass."

"No, you will not! You will come down right now or else I'm complaining to Clint!"

"Go ahead." I calmly continue to drink my coffee.

Olga clenches her fists and storms out of the lunchroom. She and the other hags can't stand that I hardly do any work anymore. If I'm not relaxing upstairs then I'm strolling around the deli tasting food; and instead of serving customers, I chat with them about fashion. I know that what really pisses the hags off is the fact that I don't care if I get into trouble. They're jealous that I don't need this job. They're jealous that I'm finally free of my dependence on this hellhole.

"Maybe you should go downstairs now." Ben gets up and pretends to clean the table. "You don't want Mr Merlon to come in here and find you doing nothing."

"Don't worry about me, Ben. I don't care."

Clint, striking as usual in a three-piece suit, comes in with Olga fuming beside him.

"See? She just sits there!" Olga points her chubby finger at me. "She has done nothing the whole morning!"

"Calm down, Olga, I'll take it from here. You get back to work." Clint waves me over. "Let's go to my office, Farina."

"Good luck, beautiful." Ben whispers to me as I begin the long march to Clint's office.

Ever since the day we fucked, I've tried my best to avoid getting stuck all alone with Clint. I don't want to be reminded of that day when I more or less sold myself. I've stopped being upset about it because life has to go on, but I'll be damned if I let it happen again. I'll never fall victim to the lure of a rich man again—not now that I'm rich myself. Except for his heart, there's nothing Clint Merlon has that I can't have.

Clint closes the door behind him and orders me to sit down. He puts up his professional façade and speaks to me like I'm just another employee. "Why aren't you downstairs and helping the girls?"

"I was gonna go in a minute." I play along with his act.

Clint relaxes his shoulders and that conceited grin—the same one he had when he nearly choked me with his penis—returns on his perfectly groomed face. "I'm not paying you a thousand dollars every week to do nothing."

"I told you I don't need your money." I turn my eyes away from his.

His clear blue eyes used to make him look so regal, so refined. Now they make him look greedy and criminal. The way he moves them up and down my body makes me feel like they're trying to pierce through my clothes and steal a view of what's incontestably and entirely mine.

Clint throws his head back and has a good laugh. "Seriously, how comfortable can you be on a maid's salary? Don't reject my generosity just because you're mad at me."

Clint pouts his lips patronizingly and I decide to put an end to his arrogance. I announce boldly, "I have a boyfriend. He's very rich, and very handsome, and he takes very good care of me."

"Really? What's the name of this rich, handsome boyfriend of yours?"

"Ali."

"What does Ali do?"

"He owns a restaurant."

"What restaurant?"

"That really nice Mediterranean place on Queen Street."

"That's weird," Clint pretends to be baffled. "Dad knows every owner in that part of the city. He's never mentioned an 'Ali.'"

"Just leave me alone," I give up. "You can stop giving me money 'cause I'm doing fine for myself now. Just let me go and finish my shift. I work eight hours a week here—just give me my seventy bucks and turn a blind eye when I add a few more minutes to my lunch. If you're so generous, just give me that."

"I should fire your cute little behind right now . . ." Clint reclines in his chair and crosses his arms behind his head. "But I need something from you."

"What do you want, Clint?"

"You see, my wife likes to spend my money on these yearly trips she calls spiritual journeys. She travels by herself for weeks, leaves me all alone at the house, doesn't call—"

"Get to the point."

"I wanna have a little fun with you while she's gone. How'd you like to come over to my house, Farina?"

I used to daydream all the time about Clint driving me through the gates to his mansion. I'm still curious about how people like him live behind their gilded doors. Although I now have the money to live as they do, there will always be an essential difference. They have rows of framed photographs lining their corridors, branches of faces that make up an old family tree with deep roots. No matter how many expensive things I hoard into my future house, my picture frames will remain empty. My money can't buy that ambience of prestige and importance.

In my dreams, Clint invited me over because I was important. He wanted me there because he respected me. In my dreams, he'd never dare to pay for me. I wasn't an affordable alternative to his wife; I was just as priceless as her.

"I'll make it worth your while," Clint continues to bid on me. "You won't need that boyfriend of yours anymore if you agree to this."

My jaw trembles with repressed anger as I attempt to articulate. I won't let Clint see me lose my cool over him. I lean in closer to him and slowly utter, "Your money can't pay me to spread my legs, Clint. It can pay me to serve sandwiches, it can pay me to be bored outta my mind, it can pay me to hate my life, but it can't pay me to be the slut your wife won't be."

Clint finally wipes off his arrogant smile and looks at me like I'm just a little more than an item for sale. "So that's why you've been acting this way? You think I only want you for sex? You think that sex is the only thing you can give me that my wife can't give me?"

"Obviously," I scoff. "I'm nothing important to you."

"You're wrong." Clint looks at me sympathetically. His icy blue eyes soften as he reaches for my hand. "You're something I've been longing for ever since my first date with a woman."

I hesitate to rest my hand in his. I search his face for any hint of insincerity. I'm both disappointed and pleased when I can't find any.

"I still remember the first day you stepped into my office and introduced yourself. I was so eager to know more about you. This innocent, beautiful, vulnerable Muslim girl from the faraway Middle East."

"I was born in Bangladesh," I correct him. "And I haven't been a Muslim for a long while."

"Those are just shallow differences, Farina—like those blonde highlights in your dark hair. The core remains. Women like you, from your side of the world, are nothing like the women here."

"What are you talking about?" I ask in total confusion. My "side of the world" for the greater part of my life has indeed been this side.

"The women in this society have forgotten their place. They're not happy to serve their men anymore." His face reddens. "I hate my wife! I only married her because she turns heads. Everyone respects you more when you've got something good-looking on your arm. They don't know how much I suffer being in the same bed with that bitch every night. She always has complaints. She always has demands. Even when I punch her pretty face, that mouth just doesn't stop running!"

Disgusted, I quickly retract my hand from Clint's grip. I don't want to touch a man who beats his wife for speaking. No matter how angry my father got at my mom's aggressive words, he never laid a hand on her. That's something my dad never did.

"Oh, don't be like the rest of these goddamn feminists here." Clint snatches my hand back. "Women from your side of the world are how women should be. Quiet, invisible, obedient, and humble enough to admit that you only have one true asset: your pussies."

Speechless, I stare at Clint while I sort out my thoughts. I'm furious that he's throwing me in the same lot as all the pathetic brown and Muslim women in the world. I've had to run away to separate myself from them. I am a feminist. Those blind Aunties in Peckville do indeed serve their men. My mother takes it upon herself to do all the housework even when my father is home and available. All the girls my age, spinelessly obedient, are happy to stay locked up inside, quiet and invisible. Clint is right.

But not entirely. I've never thought about it before, but it's dawning on me right now, right at this illuminating moment in my life, that the girls in Peckville want to be a lot more than their pussies. They work just as hard as the boys do in school. They dress to hide the curves of their breasts and hips. They wrap a veil around their heads to hide their long, seductive hair. They would never humbly admit that all they have to offer is their sexuality; they would never voluntarily reduce themselves to their sexuality. They would never join the business I witness every night, where a girl's pussy really is her one true asset. Every worker in that trade is from Clint's side of the world, if not born then raised. Too bad I can't tell him that.

Stunned by this sudden revelation, I lose all interest in Clint and whatever he has to say. I just want to leave his stuffy office and go for a long walk. I want to think about this. I try my best not to sound offended and say as casually as I can, "Wow, I didn't realize you looked at me like that, Clint. I didn't realize that women from 'my side of the world' are the only ones still happy to serve men. I guess only the women here have evolved."

"Don't take my words the wrong way, Farina. I'm giving you a compliment. You're more of a woman than my wife is." Clint still holds my hand firmly. "So please, come over and be with me while she's gone?"

Clint threatens me with his eyes as he tightens his grip. I'm over his handsomeness, his prestige, and his money. I've seen enough of it and now that he's allowed me to see beyond, all I see is a very scary man.

"I'll think about it." I jump up from my seat and force myself to smile. "Goodbye."

Today will be my last day at Nelly's Deli.

↶

Another night. Another party.

The only thing I like about this club is its bar. It's been calling to me ever since I stepped in. I push my way through all the uninteresting people and park myself by the counter. I find the cutest bartender in sight and catch his attention.

What I could really use tonight, even more than drinks, is this bartender's company. He has a little too much gel in his hair, but that can always be washed off. I hate his goatee, but that can always be snipped off. He is cute. He's indeed very cute. But he's not Ali.

"Two shots of vodka, please." I pass the bartender a bill.

He nods and flashes me a suggestive smile. His teeth are a little yellow.

"Keep the change." I guzzle the shots and quickly leave.

Sabrina and the rest are killing time in a booth with some men. Business is slow because there was a storm warning earlier today. None of the employees, except for Bambi and Kelly, are getting calls this shift. On slow nights like tonight, we just go to a club, splurge on drinks and flirt with the boys. We're not used to a single boring minute. We're all addicted to action.

I'm not keen to return to the booth. I don't want to talk to any of these guys. They're all boring yuppies who'll spend any amount of money to get laid tonight. I should just save them some time and tell them that Nikki and Jenny are for sale.

"Farina!" Sabrina calls my name and lifts her drink way up in the air. Her other hand rests on the muscular thigh of a very handsome black guy.

"Come sit over here!" She pats the seat next to hers. She's smiling. She must be drunk too.

I observe that Nikki and Jenny are not too far away, dancing with a group of college guys. They rub against their bodies, happily touching and being touched. It must be a relief to feel young and toned bodies for a change.

"This is Tony," Sabrina gestures to the man next to her. She then looks to the even better-looking one who suddenly appears next to me. "This is Tony's friend, Marcus. They both work at a law firm."

"Business law firm," Marcus corrects Sabrina and grins at me cockily. "What's your name?"

Marcus doesn't look much different than most of my ex-boyfriends. I've always had a very rigid image of what I like to see in my bed. Marcus fits all of my requirements: White, tall, and beefy with a few tattoos scattered here and there. He's my perfect man. But he's not Ali.

I'm glad that I'm interrupted by my cellphone vibrating against my thigh. I excuse myself again and quickly find the washroom.

"Hello, you've reached the Harem, how may I help you?"

"It's me, Bambi! The loser fucked me for, like, five minutes and then he came! Now I'm just sitting here. This is so awkward! I need you to pick me up right now."

"Start getting ready; we'll get you in ten."

I rush back to Sabrina, who's making out with Tony. I poke her, pull her away, and whisper into her ear, "Bambi needs to get picked up. Grab Imrana and let's go."

Sabrina must be really drunk because she doesn't budge. "Let all the girls take cabs today; I'll pay for it. You and I are spending a little more time with these guys."

I wrinkle my nose in confusion. "Since when are you willing to pay for cabs?"

"Ever since I got rich, bitch!" Sabrina laughs, moving her body to the music.

I grab Sabrina's shoulders and hold her still. "I can't stay here with these guys."

"Great. You've gone Muslim."

"No," I glance away, "I'm kinda with somebody."

Sabrina doesn't look so jolly anymore. She stops dancing, returns to her stiff, overburdened self. She stares at me with her steely eyes, and I can tell that she feels betrayed.

"You been dating somebody and you don't even tell me?"

"I'll tell you about it later. I'm leaving now. I can't work the phones in this loud place." I pat her arm to calm her down and prevent causing a scene. She'll thank me when she sobers up. She's the one who always stresses the importance of appearing professional in front of employees.

Sabrina continues to stare at me for a while before she nods vacantly, "Fine. Take a cab to the apartment. Imrana and I will meet you there in a few hours."

"How are you guys getting home?"

"I'm good to drive." Before turning around and walking away, she says sharply, "Don't pretend like you actually give a fuck about me!"

I'm pissed at her, but I understand her. Best friends don't keep quiet about boyfriends. She probably thinks she's not that important to me. That's bullshit, of course. The only reason I didn't tell her about Ali is because I didn't want her to make fun of me. I guess that makes me not only a bad friend but also a terrible girlfriend.

I sigh and make my way out of the club with a very unpleasant taste in my mouth. I never thought relationships could be more complicated than making money.

There are several cabs outside, but I decide to walk a few blocks. I miss being able to walk alone with my thoughts. I forgot that there's another side to night time than just the one with flashing blue lights, loud music, drunk people, and thrilling danger. There's also the one with mysterious darkness, peaceful silence, reflective loners, and safety. Now that I know them both, I think I like one side more than the other.

As I continue down the road and reach the main intersection, I hear a car stop abruptly beside me. A chubby Uncle rolls down the window of his rusty minivan and asks me with a strong accent, "Chester Street, which direction?"

I can see a veiled woman in the passenger seat and a veiled preteen girl in the backseat. The woman's yelling at the man in Urdu, I think. She looks really angry. The girl looks frightened.

The man turns to the woman and yells even louder. The girl struggles to turn against her seatbelt as she fixes her sight on me. Her eyes wide and her lips parted, she looks at my cleavage, my heels, and my tight miniskirt with tremendous interest.

"Excuse me," I say, breaking up the fight. "You just have to go straight down, turn left, and keep driving until you see the sign for it."

"Ha! I am never wrong!" The Uncle says to the Auntie before they both resume their yelling.

The girl puts one hand against the window and tries to catch a better view of my purse. I hold it up for her to see and she smiles gratefully. She keeps her eyes locked on me as the car zooms away. What the hell is she so envious of?

NINE

It's eleven in the morning, five hours after closing time, and I haven't been able to get a minute of sleep. Sabrina and Imrana didn't come home yesterday. Their phones are off and Nikki and Jenny have no clue where they are. I shouldn't have let Sabrina drive her car. I should've just stuck around with them. I should've asked her to give me her keys and if she refused I should've beaten her unconscious and dragged her body to a cab. Even that'd be better than just leaving her and Imrana's safety to luck.

I've pointlessly called their cellphones every thirty minutes for the past five hours or so. There's not much more I can do but sit here and stare at the door, pray that the knob will turn soon. Although I feel like an idiot pointing my cupped hands to the sky and talking to myself aloud, I continue to close my eyes and pray. Praying doesn't seem so ridiculous when you're hopeless. I know that God has no reason to listen to the hopes of a criminal, and so I don't beg—I barter. "Take all the money back," I insist. "I don't want the fucking money. Just give me my friends and I swear I'll get an honest job."

Heaven must be calling my bluff because suddenly I hear a knock. I look above as if expecting to see an angel on my ceiling, but then get back to my senses and run to the door. I don't miss Imrana and Sabrina anymore; I'm furious at them for keeping me in terror the whole night. I swing the door open, screaming, "Where the hell have you two—" and nearly swallow my tongue. It's not Sabrina and Imrana. It's my mother and Imrana's mother.

"Where's Imrana?" Mrs Ahmed asks me firmly but politely

in Bengali. Her half-open eyes are bloodshot with bluish pockets beneath them. Strands of her frizzy, uncombed hair bravely poke out of her sloppily wrapped hijab. "Please tell me where Imrana is."

"Tell your Auntie right now, Farina." My mom is not nearly as polite as Mrs Ahmed. She glares as me threateningly like she always did before using the dreaded wooden spatula on me. "You girls have gone too far. We're going to stop this today."

I can hardly comprehend what they're saying because I'm focused on keeping them out of the apartment. My heart fluttering in my chest, I stretch my arms and make myself as broad as I can in order to block the door. Luckily I'm a good bit taller than either of them, so they can't get a full view of the living room. There are way too many things inside that they'll want to interrogate me about. Besides all the expensive stuff, are empty alcohol bottles and cigarette butts lying around.

"I don't know where she is," I say nervously in my broken Bengali as I quickly look down at myself to check what I'm wearing. I'm relieved that I changed out of my club wear and into my pyjamas earlier this morning.

"You do know where she is!" My mother shouts as she puts her arms around a sobbing Mrs Ahmed. "Let us in because we're not leaving until you tell us."

I stand frozen with my arms shielding the doorway. I can't let them in no matter how angry my mom gets. If she catches any hint of me making money illegally, she'll either kill me or physically force me back to my father's dungeon. I coldly ignore Mrs Ahmed's agony and assert myself in English, "I'm busy with something. You guys have to leave right now."

My mother glowers at me before she simply pushes my arm away. She steps into my apartment without any more talk and continues to comfort Mrs Ahmed. "Come in, Bhabhi."

I shake my head at the futility of teaching my mother that I'm an adult who deserves respect. I quickly close the bedroom door so at least she won't find my massive wardrobe. I frantically scan the living room for anything she shouldn't see. By the time I notice the empty vodka bottle next to the couch, it's too late.

My mom helps Mrs Ahmed sit down before she starts about the bottle. "What is this? This is what you do here? Drinking? Disgusting!"

I sit down and stare at my hands. There's no point being on edge anymore because she's found out the worst that I'll let her find out. She'll never know about the Harem. Even if she accuses me of something to do with an escort agency, I'll deny it until I'm blue in the face. Let her bring it on.

"Disgusting!" My mother hurls the bottle across the room, shattering it into a million pieces. I've never seen her so full of rage as not to care about appearances. She looks around at all the fabulous things I own and screams at me, "Such a big TV? Such a nice desk? A computer, too? How did a little girl like you get all this? What are you doing for money?"

"I've already told you on the phone," I say with a face as unmoving as concrete. "My catering job pays great."

"You think you're so much smarter than me?" My mother grits her teeth and tries to intimidate the truth out of me. "Your father and I have worked at a hundred catering jobs since our arrival to this hellish country! None of them pay enough to buy all these things in just a few months!"

No matter how thick the plaster on my face, my mom sees right through it. She knows very well that I'm lying. She stares at me aggressively, challenging me to give her an explanation that makes sense.

I flash a foxy smile and calmly lie, "I bought it all on credit."

"You liar! I've raised a liar!" She yells out along with a lot of Bengali profanities that I don't know the meanings of.

"What is the point of yelling at her now?" Mrs Ahmed stops crying for a minute and motions for my mother to stop screaming.

"All our lives, we've just yelled at them all night and day, and what did it do? They're gone. We lost them."

My mom suddenly remembers that we aren't alone in the room. She shuts her eager lips and parks herself next to Mrs Ahmed. She pats the wailing woman's back as she collects herself and then asks me rather nicely, "Where is Imrana? We know that you're the first person she would go to. Have some sympathy for your Auntie and just tell her where her daughter is."

"Those are her shoes!" Mrs Ahmed says between sobs and points. Stupid Imrana just had to take one of my pairs last night.

"Okay, fine, she's staying here with me," I admit. "But I don't know where she is."

"She just left without telling you?" Mrs Ahmed's tone gets more and more confrontational. "Was she here yesterday?"

I decide to cooperate because I'm just as worried about Imrana as she is. I'd rather rat on Imrana than waste any more time sitting here and not looking for her. "Yes, Auntie, she was here. She went to a party and she hasn't come back yet. She hasn't called me either."

Mrs Ahmed gasps at the word "party" and her sobbing gets louder.

"And you didn't go to this party?" My mother attacks me.

I tell them the truth about leaving early, but I don't mention Sabrina or the rich guys. My mom hates Sabrina. Imrana's mom hates Sabrina. Every mother in Peckville hates Sabrina.

"You left her there with Sabrina Jahan, didn't you?" My mom sees right through me yet again. "How many times have I told you to avoid Sabrina? She's not a good girl. Everybody knows that."

Mrs Ahmed nods in agreement and adds snootily, "She has no class. When she used to live here, she'd never greet me when she saw me. She'd always just walk right by with a boy holding her hand. And it was a different boy every time!"

"She has no future. She doesn't even care about school," my

mom says, demeaning my best friend. "I heard that she didn't even apply to any universities."

My mom and Mrs Ahmed keep condemning Sabrina, as if Imrana and I were so much better. This is what the parents of the holier-than-thou club do in their spare time: point their judgemental fingers at any kid but their own. I've been a favourite victim of this shit ever since I moved out. I've caught Aunties around Peckville, grown women who should have better things to do, whisper and laugh behind my back. I've never said anything to them because I know better than to speak my language while on a foreigner's turf. I've accepted it out there in the neighbourhood, but I won't accept it in my own living room.

Incensed, I shoot up from my seat and open the door wide. "If you wanna talk bad about Sabrina, go do it outside in the hall!"

My mom shakes her head at me disappointedly. "Why are you so angry? Who is that girl to you? For her sake, you're ready to kick your own mother out of your house."

"She's my best friend!" I scream at the top of my lungs. "You dare judge my best friend to my face! You don't even know her!"

"We know all we need to know about her," my mom says decisively. "We won't let you associate with her. She's a very immoral girl."

"How do you know I'm not just as immoral as her?" I challenge my mom's narrow views of good and bad.

I'm no less of a pimp than Sabrina is. The Harem may have been Sabrina's idea, but I sure didn't hesitate to go along with it. I'm the one who sells bodies; all she does is drive them around. I'm the one who flirts with strangers on the phone; all she does is find out where they live. I'm the one who gives up my apartment, the symbol of my freedom, for the sake of money; all she gives up is some of her time. If Sabrina's immoral, then I'm downright satanic.

"You are nothing like her. You have a family. You grew up with a lot of love. You don't know Sabrina's family's story because you were too young to understand." My mom looks at her lap solemnly as Mrs Ahmed tells the story:

"Her father would beat her mother black and blue almost every night. I visited Jahan Bhabhi a lot when she first moved here. There were always bruises or cuts on her body. One time I found her with her lower lip completely torn. She laughed about it. She thought it was funny. He'd beaten her so much that there just weren't any feelings or sense left in her. She was a cold and crazy woman. She didn't know how to raise a child."

I sit down again and pay close attention. "You guys knew about the beatings and you did nothing?" I keep my contemptuous gaze on my mother. "You should've called the cops and put him in jail."

My mother scoffs. "We were also new to the country at that time. We hardly knew English. We didn't know that the police here cared about husbands beating their wives. It's not taken so seriously by the police back home."

"So you just let Sabrina watch her mom getting battered everyday . . ."

"We tried to make Sabrina turn to God. If anyone needed God's mercy, it was that poor little girl." Mrs Ahmed feels better. "I encouraged Jahan Bhabhi to make Sabrina do all the prayers and go to mosque after school. I even picked her up myself every Sunday to take her to Arabic school. Our plan was working well for a while. Sabrina was a bit rude, but she was on the Islamic path. But it didn't last very long."

"Only at ten years old, her misfortunes became her. She talked back to adults. She questioned God. She shamelessly begged her mother to divorce her father." My mother looks despondent. "How broken must a family be for a ten-year-old child to beg her mom to divorce her dad?"

"Did her mom ever consider a divorce?" I ask, hopeful for a positive answer.

"Never!" My mom exclaims indignantly.

"Of course not." With a bitter accent, I mock the explanation I expect my mom to give me—the one she always gave me when I told her to divorce my father: "We're Muslim and we're Bangladeshi. We don't divorce because we're so damn holy and traditional."

"No, we're women and we're poor. We don't divorce because people have not designed this world for single mothers." My mom shocks me with her nonreligious answer. "Any pain we take from our husbands, we take because of necessity, not tradition. We take their violence and we take their angry words, and we give our children the home they need, the food they need, and the clothes they need. Our children will never have to say that the government was their father."

I stare at my mom with awe. She's actually speaking to me like I'm an intelligent adult. She's actually explaining something to me without threatening me with God's wrath. I'm probably wrong, but it feels like she's giving me respect. For the first time in my life, I feel like my mom respects me.

I feel comfortable enough now to confront her, "What about happiness, Mom? Do you give your kids happiness by sacrificing yourselves like that? Don't you think it hurts your daughters to watch you get hurt? Why else would a girl beg her mom to divorce her dad?"

"I think Sabrina knows very little about her father." My mom uses Sabrina's name although we clearly aren't talking about her anymore. This is about us.

I see the regret in my mom's eyes as she says to me, "I think if Sabrina gave her mom a chance to tell her more about her dad's history, Sabrina would have sympathy for him. She wouldn't want to just leave him behind. He loved her very much whether she believes it or not."

"He sure didn't show it." I gnaw at the flesh around my nails, containing my rage, hurt, and frustration. "He was never there.

He ignored her most of the time, like she was just the rug beneath his feet."

"There is an explanation for that," my mom pleads with me. "If Sabrina would just give her mother a chance to explain, she'd understand everything."

"She's had eighteen years to explain. Why didn't she?"

Tears trickle down my mom's tender cheeks. "She's made mistakes. She was so busy working that she couldn't see those mistakes. But she understands them now and she will fix everything if Sabrina just gives her a chance. If she just comes back home and listens to her mom, her mom will fix everything."

Mrs Ahmed, too lost in her worries to understand what we're talking about, interrupts our moment. "The point is that Sabrina grew up with both her parents paying no attention to her. Once the lung cancer took her father, she lost any chance of having a normal family. She never learned how to bond with or care for others: the things one naturally first learns in one's home. She doesn't care about anyone because she thinks that no one cares about her. She cunningly takes advantage of anyone who loves her. She always took advantage of my Imrana."

Before I can defend Sabrina, we all turn our attention to the giggles coming from the hall. The idiots sure picked the best time to return.

Sabrina and Imrana step inside with snags and alcohol stains all over their revealing dresses. Imrana's eyes widen at the sight of her mother. She takes a step back as if readying herself to take off, but then changes her mind and marches in fearlessly. "Go away! I'm not going back with you!"

Mrs Ahmed shoots up from the couch and eyes Imrana's tight tube dress with a look of sheer disbelief. "You've been outside all night dressed like that? You could've been raped! What will people think? You look like a whore!"

Sabrina rests against the door frame and watches the drama

like an unconcerned fly on the wall. Yawning, she shuts the door before disappearing into my bedroom.

Mrs Ahmed grabs Imrana's arm and begins to drag her away. Imrana twists herself loose and shoves her mom so violently that she falls on the floor and slams her head against the living room table.

"Leave me the hell alone, you bitch!" Imrana shrieks as her mom cries out in pain. "I'll look like a whore if I want to!"

My mom helps Mrs Ahmed up and I hold Imrana back by placing myself in front of her. Like a fish caught out of water, she shimmies wildly and frenziedly behind me. I didn't know that timid and shy Imrana had it in her to be this angry. In her rage, she scratches me, and tries to push me out of her way. No matter how fierce her clawing, I stay put because I know she'll do something horrible if I let her free. Her sharp nails scratching me all over, I beg Mrs Ahmed to leave before something worse happens.

A dizzy Mrs Ahmed vows to return as she's led out of the apartment by my mom. Imrana stops trembling as soon as her mom leaves her view. She takes her hands off of me and plonks herself into the couch, breathing heavily.

"Wait." I stop my mom before she leaves. "Will you be alone home next Sunday?"

"Yes. Why?"

"I want to come over. I want you to tell me about Dad."

The life behind my mom's eyes resurrects. She gives me a smile and signals her approval. I hold on to the image of her beautiful smile long after she shuts the door. It feels like a lifetime that I've longed for just a glimpse of it.

"Where were you?" I turn to Imrana.

"Paradise," she says, oblivious of what just happened with her mother, and rolls her eyes with glee. "Those guys took us to a party at their place. You should've been there. All the drink, dope, and dick you could ever want. I never felt so free in my entire life."

"Well, maybe I could've dropped by if you picked up one of my million calls."

"We were so drunk," Imrana laughs, "we both lost our phones."

"That's not funny," I snap. I'm a lot more annoyed than impressed. I didn't stay awake for a whole day just to hear about how much fun they had.

"We can always get new phones." Imrana puts her legs up on the table and relaxes. "Lighten up. Life is good."

I jeer at her before I give her a wake-up call: "As long as you're living ten floors above your mom, life ain't so good. She'll be back again soon to get you. Trust me, they don't give up so easily."

"She won't find me here anymore. I'm moving into a motel today."

"I'm not letting you sleep in some dirty motel. Besides, how are you going to pay for it? We haven't even discussed your new percentage yet."

Imrana's eyes dance around mine, avoiding any direct contact. "Actually, Sabrina discussed that with me last night."

"Without me there?" I frown.

"Don't worry. My new position won't affect your cut." Imrana slouches down and peeks cautiously at me and says, "I've decided that I'm gonna be an escort."

"What?" I can't believe what she's just said.

"Look, I know you and Sabrina need all the money you're getting from the agency. I know that I don't have my driver's licence and that I'd totally suck on the phone. There really is no other work for me except the ads." She sighs. "Sabrina said she'll let me keep two-hundred dollars for every appointment. That's a lot more than the other girls. I really need that type of money right now."

"So this was all Sabrina's idea?" I feel the veins in my forehead throb as I scream, "Sabrina told you to do this?"

"No, no—it was entirely my choice." Imrana sits up straight, trying to convince me she's confident this is what she wants. "I've been thinking about doing it for a long time."

"No, you haven't!" I pace up and down the room with panic and frustration. "You told me you wanted to finish school and be a nurse!"

"Fuck, Farina, stop yelling at me!" Imrana presses her palms on the sides of her forehead and circles them around to ease her apparent headache. "You know I never wanted to be a nurse. It's just another thing I had to do to make my parents happy. I'm done being the good little loser who just takes orders from her parents. I wanna move out, get my own life, and just be free."

I bang my fist on the table: "You really think that selling yourself to strangers is freedom?"

I think about how the employees spend their days. Sure, they've got nobody to tell them what time to start work or what time to end. They can go weeks without work if they want. They've got enough free time to party every single night—to just party away whatever dream they had once upon a time. They can drink and dance further and further away from their dream as the sand races through the hourglass. Is that freedom?

They've got more money than they need and they can spend it all on things, things, and more things. But things always lose their spark no matter how happy they once made you or how much they impressed your neighbours. All things eventually become nothing. Dust. These girls can have a limitless number of things in exchange for what can't be stored in the attic or sold in the garage: their physical and mental health. Is that freedom?

Maybe all the strict laws that govern us girls in Peckville are there for a reason. Maybe our fathers and brothers were always just a pack of wolves protecting us from another pack of wolves. It's a big world out there and anybody can get lost without a map. Maybe, for all these years, our parents were just trying to hand us a map.

"You don't know what you're getting into," I tell Imrana. "I'm on the phone with these perverts all the time. They talk about girls like they're nothing more than bodies to be fucked. They ask about your tits and your ass like they're buying pillows. How big? How soft? How firm? How do they bounce? You do this and you become merchandise, you understand? You become a fucking thing. They see nothing beyond your skin."

"All girls are just skin anyway." She begins to speak so quietly that I have to lean towards her to hear what she has to say. "You know, I'm turning nineteen in a few weeks and I've never had a guy hold my hand and walk with me at the mall or park. Never had any guy give me a Valentine, or buy me a birthday gift, or say anything sweet. Why? Because I don't look good enough for all that effort."

"That's bullshit. You get enough love from guys. I see them stare at you all the time."

"Yeah, of course they give me love now. I spend at least an hour every morning finding an outfit, straightening my hair, and doing my make-up just right. An hour of work for just a few glances from guys I don't even find hot." She chuckles sardonically. "I couldn't get anybody to look at me twice in high school."

"You were so shy in high school. It was just hard for guys to approach you." I try to sound as convincing as I can with my white lie.

"Do you have any idea what it felt like to be 'that ugly, chubby dark girl who hangs out with beautiful Sabrina and Farina'?" Imrana begins to whimper. "Do you know what it feels like to be used by every guy you've ever loved? They pretend like they love you too just so they can fuck you. And then, when you cry about it, they laugh at you and tell you how amazingly dumb you are. How amazingly dumb you are for thinking that a guy would love somebody as fat and ugly as you?"

I grab Imrana's hand and I don't let go. She goes on,

"I used to hate Sabrina for a while. At least you did some work in school; she did nothing but exercise all the time. She failed English once, calculus twice, she was rude to everybody and yet all the boys treated her like she was a goddess." Imrana tries hard to stop crying. "At first, I hated her because all that attention just wasn't fair, but then I realized what I know now: the only girls who get love in this man's world are the beautiful ones. I admire Sabrina. No guy ever uses her. No guy ever tosses her aside after he gets what he wants."

"You really think that only beautiful girls get love?"

"Yeah," Imrana wipes away her tears and drops my hand. "I can hide behind all this sticky shit on my face forever, but it won't change the fact that no guy wants something serious with me. Sabrina made a really good point about this yesterday. She said that it makes no sense for me to be used for sex and not get anything in return. At least, as an escort, I'll get all the money I need and want right now."

I feel a rage towards Sabrina, but I can't say or do anything to act on it. This is a whole new type of rage. A passionless rage, if that makes any sense. I'm not so mad at something that she did that I can point to and hunt down; I'm simply filled with fury from the tip of my toenails to the end of my hair strands. The rage is so heavy that I can't move.

"What else did Sabrina say?" I bring myself to ask.

"She said there's nothing more exciting than sleeping with a complete stranger. She's absolutely right," Imrana says with a nod. "When we fucked those guys last night, after just a few hours of chat, I felt such a rush. I felt so sexy."

I study Imrana's face, hoping for an indication that she's been tricked or drugged or threatened into wanting this. There's nothing but a raw expression of excitement and readiness. This is what she wants. This is her first major choice outside of her parents' home.

"Just be here for me, Farina." Imrana smiles at me. "Like you've always been."

"Of course." I smile back at her reluctantly as I gaze at her inno-cent dimples. "Let's just get some sleep now."

Imrana stretches her legs out on the couch and lets out a hearty yawn. I close the window curtains and go to my bedroom. I open the door and find Sabrina sprawled out on my bed, sleeping like a newborn. There's not a single worry in her cute curly-haired head.

I shake Sabrina's shoulder until she awakens. I wait until she's alert enough to look into my eyes and then I ask her, "What the hell did you do?"

Sabrina moves back and makes space for me. She whispers with a grin and a wink, "I told you I'd get us a South Asian by the end of this month."

TEN

"So she takes her clothes off and I'm like 'damn, wow'," Mustafa says and kicks the back of my seat so suddenly that I jump with surprise. "I ain't ever seen a hotter body," he adds.

He and two more of Ali's Eastside friends are sitting behind us in Ali's car, laughing and bragging about all the hot "sluts" they've slept with. My presence doesn't bother them. Until I marry Ali and become his sacred wife, I'm just some irrelevant chick that hangs out with him. The holier-than-thou club doesn't keep girlfriends; their women are either wives or nothing. These clowns don't respect me.

"But then I get started on her huge tits and I swear I feel something in my mouth when I'm done."

"What?" The other two clowns ask in unison.

"I pull it out of my mouth, hold it to the light and—holy fuck—it's a hair!"

They fall back in their seats and roll with laughter. Mustafa kicks my seat repeatedly and the other two, totally oblivious to the fact that he's driving, slap Ali's shoulders to get his attention. I wonder how somebody like him can be friends with these losers. I bet he's like them when I'm not around.

"Just ignore them," Ali tells me with a tight smile. "You're so quiet tonight. Is something wrong?"

I shake my head, not looking at him, not wanting to talk to him. I don't feel like talking to anybody.

"Put your seatbelt on."

I shake my head again.

"Did I do something?"

I finally turn and look at his worried face. I smile at him appreciatively to let him know that he's not the problem. I'm just not so wet for him tonight. All that's on my mind is Imrana—especially what she said about only beautiful girls finding love.

"Her sister's still hotter," one of the clowns argues once he's done wheezing with laughter.

"Yeah," the other agrees, "lighter, taller, and not as fat."

"She's not fat," Mustafa defends his lover, "and you need a little cushion for the pushin' anyway."

While the three of them continue to debate about the so-called perfect body, I feel a sharp pain in my stomach. They're literally making me sick in my stomach. Their talk reminds me of my daily phone conversations with Pigs. Much like these bored and immature boys, I also talk about girls' bodies like they're products to be appraised. The only difference is that I actually put a real price tag on their beauty. These guys assign an invisible rating that directly reflects how much a girl deserves love, attention and admiration. They are exactly the attributes that Imrana was crying about.

"Are we there yet?" I ask Ali loudly so that hopefully his friends will shut up.

Ali nods and turns into the parking lot of the Eastside beach. This is the dirtiest beach in the city but we had to come to this one because his friends have to meet some customers. All three are drug dealers.

Ali finds an empty spot and stops the car. He turns to his friends and orders them to get out to do their business. Once they leave, he grabs my hand and asks forcefully, "What's bothering you?"

I realize that he's not going to loosen his grip and so I give up and ask him glumly, "Why are you with me?"

He chuckles and makes a face at my dumb question. I do hate the sound of me asking this sappy soap-opera question, but it has to be asked.

"Everybody in Peckville talks shit about me. I'm never getting a degree. I don't have God in my life. I'm not Ms Popular. I've got nothing in common with you."

Ali seems as uncomfortable as I am discussing this topic, but he still manages to reply seriously, "I think you and me have a lot in common."

"Like what? A nice face?"

"That's one thing," he jokes.

"Why won't you just fuck me and have your fun?" I ask him with a suspicious stare. "Is it really because God says not to? Or am I just too beautiful to ruin?"

Ali remains quiet and stares distantly at the dark beach and ponders his answer. After a long minute, he sighs and unlocks my door. "Let's walk and get some air."

We get out of the car and meet by its hood. He curls his pinkie around my ring finger and gently kisses the back of my hand. His eyes look down and meet mine and I'm both surprised and elated at their message. He bends down slightly and I instantly raise myself up onto my tiptoes. I'm filled with joyous disbelief as I feel the stubble on his face prickle the skin around my lips. Without thinking twice, I part my lips to welcome his, but I feel nothing on my tongue but the wind. He doesn't kiss me.

"I'm not with you just because you look good." Ali gazes at my lips with such longing in his brown eyes, but then forces himself to look away. He begins to head towards the beach and I tag along, disappointed and curious.

The govern-men won't bother to add a boardwalk to the tiny beach that only the city's poorest visit, and so we trek through the dirty sand with our shoes on. We walk cautiously at a slow and steady pace, veering away from broken beer bottles and used needles. Neither of us really wants to continue our sentimental conversation, so we avoid it by walking in complete silence.

When there are no more directions to cover, we stop and sit

down on one of the large flat rocks in front of the lake. We can hear Ali's friends and their customers laughing hysterically somewhere in the distance. They must've used their own product because there's no natural reason for them to laugh so genuinely. It's not possible to laugh with your heart when you live your life under constant threat—I would know. These guys make their money in the deadly corners of ghettos; their greatest enemy is the armed and unbeatable police; their only friends are their moms who of course have to go into that good night and leave them all alone one day. Happiness escaped their repertoire of emotions a long time ago, and it's now just attainable in dreams induced by a favourite drug.

But why, then, do I feel something like happiness sitting here next to Ali?

Ali only has three syllables for his friends and he states them in the driest of tones: "Time-wasters."

"Not everybody has a life as perfect as yours," I defend my fellow users as I pull my knees in and hug them tightly.

"Oh please," Ali dismisses my point sharply. "My dad hits me when he feels like it, my mom's always on my case, and my lil bro comes first no matter how bad my day is—now should I go and kill my future?"

"You don't get it," I shake my head. "It's not about killing the future, it's about killing the moment. Some moments are too painful or too enraging or just too mind-numbing to bear. You just need something to distract you, and that something isn't always drugs."

I reflect on my own words as my mind wanders back to Imrana. Maybe her decision to become an Employee wasn't based entirely on her need and want of money. Maybe it's the unusual lifestyle that comes attached with the job that won her over. All the glamour, partying and new faces are sure to be a distraction from her dark moments of insecurity. Maybe she's just out to kill the memories of multiple rejections by making herself available to be wanted by just about anybody. Attention can be like a drug—but what do I know? I'm just a little insignificant Paki girl.

"You're totally right about drugs not being the only distraction." Ali's musing eyes see right through me and find my intentions. "Sex is a big one too, right?"

"I guess."

"You ask me why I won't have sex with you, but you don't ask yourself why you wanna have sex with me." Ali smiles at me apologetically and asserts, "I ain't gonna be your drug, Farina."

"So what the hell are you doing sitting here with me?" I raise my voice in irritation. "Are you really that shallow, Ali? You know my dirty intentions and yet you stick with me just because you like the size of my boobs! What the hell is wrong with you boys? It's only about the outside! Girls are more than just looks—we're fucking human beings!"

"Calm down; you're acting crazy," Ali pleads, and laughs nervously at my outburst.

When I'm calm, he begins to explain, "I wouldn't risk my parents' trust, spit on our country's traditions, and compromise with God just 'cause I like the size of your boobs. I'm sitting here with you because I really like you. I know I shouldn't be here. I know I'm not supposed to have a girl, but feelings don't come with a steering wheel."

I stare him down, still unsatisfied with his answer. "What do you like so much about me?"

"I like who you are. I think you're a good person."

The honesty in his voice gives me goose bumps.

"I respect you way too much to just see your outside." Ali glides his arms around my waist and pulls me in closer to him. "I wish you'd have the same respect for me. You're putting me in the same bin as white dudes. Just because the TV says it's normal for guys to be dogs doesn't make it so. Not all of us live to get off. You and me have only been together a few months; we ain't married; we ain't planning on making a baby anytime soon; so what's the point of jumping into bed? I'm in no hurry. My answer is that simple."

I've been away from the ordinary world for so long now that I've forgotten that not everybody with a penis is a Pig. I feel terrible that I actually saw a Pig in Ali. I forgot that he always treats me like a whole person. He listens more than he looks. He talks more than he touches. Indeed, he respects me more than I respect him.

I'm the one who leads a secret life and shields it from him by telling him a million lies. He never knows where I really am. He never knows what I'm really doing. He doesn't know a thing about all the harm I cause every night just to pay for my shiny shoes and my fitted jackets.

And yet he calls or leaves sweet text messages on my cellphone every single day because he thinks that I'm "a good person."

I can't stand to look at his face when I confess, "I'm not a good person, Ali."

"Yes, you are. I've done some thinking, and you are." He smiles at me. "All those Peckville people who talk shit about you don't even know you. They're so quick to judge that they forget their own sins. They totally forget the change in their own behaviour now that they got into university. I know people who used to donate their hard-earned money to the mosque who never even come by anymore. They're now drinking, clubbing, and spending their student loans on preppy clothes. They'll give up their histories, their principles, and even their compassion just to fit in and get some cushy jobs. They're all about the money."

I lower my head with shame and guilt and ask him, "How do you know I'm not all about the money?"

"How can you be about the money if you're sitting here with me?" he explains, and puts his arm around my waist. "I've got nothing to give you but hugs. I can't help you out and it hurts me because I don't like you working two jobs just to survive, Farina.

You could really use a guy with money right now, but you've decided to be mine. You're always sweet to me. You're faithful. You're honest."

My voice breaks when I ask, "I'm honest?"

Ali goes on and on about how much he trusts me. He praises me for my openness about everything. When I can't stand to listen anymore, I push him away gently and tell him to be quiet. I spring up from the rock and walk ahead quickly. I need air.

Guilt is choking me.

He comes running to catch up and forces me to hold on to him tightly. His gentle hands caress my back and he says softly, "Please tell me what's wrong. I can tell that something's very wrong."

"I'm just worried about the future," I lie—but not entirely. "I don't know where my life's going. I don't know if things are ever gonna be normal. I just don't know what my future is."

"You're gonna be fine," Ali whispers into my ear and I devour the familiar scent of him. "I'll make sure that you're fine. I'll be your future."

I've never wanted to kiss Ali as badly as I do right now. I think that I should show him some respect by asking to kiss him, but on a second thought, I won't ask because he's mine. He's mine and I'll let the Harem go before I'll ever let him go. After I have enough money for my condo, I'll leave this immoral life behind and be his. Honestly.

"I really, really like you," I say before I kiss him passionately.

When Ali finally pulls his lips away from me for a breath of air, he whispers, "I really, really like you too."

Instead of laughing or crying with utter bliss, I grab Ali's hand and start toward the parking lot. "Let's hurry up and get back to the car. Your friends are waiting."

I can't give into my emotions just yet. I can't give into my conscience just yet. I have to be stronger than my guilt if I want that condo. I have to bear the pangs just a little longer if I want to get out of Peckville.

ELEVEN

I don't want to watch this sordid movie, but I can't shut my mind's eye. I see the hairy back of a man, a faceless man, sitting at the edge of his bed as Imrana undresses for him. Right now, she's all alone in a hotel room with a Pig. I see this stranger's large grasping hands grabbing and feeling her naked body. His weight crushes her as he glides on top of her, licking her face like a starved dog. Whether she's ready or not, he pushes himself inside her. He does it again and again and again. I can't quite make out her expression. Does she feel excited or angry or has she just emptied herself of all emotion? It doesn't matter. Whatever she's feeling, she's still being used. That's my friend I see being used like a fucking pay toilet.

"Pick it up!" Sabrina wakes me up from my trance and shifts my attention to my ringing cellphone.

"Hi, you've reached the Harem," I mumble flatly. "How may I help you?"

"Good evening, do any of your girls offer Greek?"

I hate how incredibly civil and passive Pigs are on the phone. This one's asking for a "Greek" like it's just an innocent service he's interested in. He wants to stick his cock up a stranger's asshole and he has the audacity to behave like a normal customer of a normal business. I'd rather he just speak to me crudely and rudely. At least then he'd admit that this is far from a normal business.

"Yeah, give me a second, I'll check for you," I slur with deliberate bitterness.

I can't take much more of this life. No amount of alcohol is strong enough to help anymore. Everything about this world is beginning to irk, anger, and depress me. No matter how well it compensates, I can't forgive it for stealing Imrana. Every second that I spend with my phone in my hand, waiting for calls from men who want to use her, I'm tortured with guilt.

Somewhere in the back of my mind, I'm continuously counting down the dollars and the days until I can finally return to the world out there. I can't wait to hide away in my new condo, far away from both Peckville and Pigs. I'll spend most of my time with Ali. Maybe I'll ask him to move in with me one day. I know Allah doesn't like unmarried couples living together, so maybe, one day, I'll marry Ali. I really wouldn't mind marrying Ali.

I scan my notebook when Africa suddenly pokes my shoulder from the backseat. "Did he ask for anal?"

"Uh-huh."

"I offer that now."

"Okay," I utter with surprise and note it down. "Are you sure?"

"Of course she's sure," Sabrina interrupts. "I think that's a great move, Africa. It'll really help your business."

"I know," Africa tries to smile away her obvious nervousness. She says to me timidly, "You can also add cum-in-mouth."

"Only Africa offers Greek," I reluctantly tell the Pig.

"Fabulous. May I book an hour with her as soon as possible?"

I let Sabrina know the Pig's address and she runs a red light speeding towards it.

Africa's the only Employee who's been sitting idly in the backseat for the past two hours. I wish she didn't have to go because I'm not ready to be alone in the car with Sabrina. I'm still pissed at her. We have a lot to talk about and, frankly, I don't want to talk to her yet.

Africa seems tense once we reach her client's neighbourhood. Sabrina unlocks her door, but she stays put. She stares at the client's house as she gnaws on her fingernails anxiously.

"Are you ready?" Sabrina urges her to leave.

Africa nods, takes a deep breath, and leaves the car.

If I didn't know Africa's situation, I'd deem her stupid for doing what she's about to do. A hundred-something dollars may seem like a fortune for a few minutes of pain, but how many nights will it be physically possible to work? On a weekly or monthly basis, she'll be making peanuts for selling her asshole. She won't make any more money per year than the govern-men's construction workers. Sure, construction workers lift heavy things until their biceps ache and their backs burn, but at least their rectums and their dignities remain intact.

But dignity is a luxury that only specific people can afford. It's not that easy for girls like Africa to choose an alternative job that pays enough to raise two kids. I sure have never seen a young mother in construction. When she first realized that she had to raise her twins all by herself, she probably knew that this industry was her best bet. She probably even knew that, because of her skin colour, she'd have to abuse herself much worse than others in order to match their pay. Africa isn't stupid. What she's giving up now is just what she was too dignified to give up before.

Imrana will never have to do anything as painful and dangerous as anal sex. She's high in demand. I feel a gush of relief once I realize that, but then my guilt returns more ferociously than before. I'm not strong enough to lie to myself anymore. I admit to myself what I've known since that first day Sabrina told me about this business. I admit to myself that Africa is somebody's Imrana. All the Employees are somebody's Imrana.

"Hey!" I call out to Africa as she walks away from us.

Africa stops and turns around. Involuntarily, I imagine that I'm one of her seven-year-olds and that I know what's about to happen. I can see myself sprinting towards her and locking my arms around her knee, crying and begging her not to go into that stranger's house. I tell her that I'll go hungry for another week. I'll wear the same clothes for the rest of my life. I'll never ask for another toy again. I'll get a job myself as long as she doesn't go into that stranger's house.

"What is it?" Africa asks me, motioning for me to hurry up.

"Call me if something goes wrong. Anything at all. Just call me."

"Yeah, I know that." Africa rolls her eyes at me and continues to walk away.

"What the hell is going on with you? You're all—stupid like you're in love." Sabrina puts the car in park, reclines in her seat and lights a cigarette. She's ready to talk. "You're in love, aren't you?"

I want to ignore Sabrina, but the neighbourhood is so quiet that all I hear is her breathing. I light me a cigarette and soon we're inhaling and exhaling in unison. It's just she and I in this lonely place. It's always been just she and I in some lonely place until now.

"How could you do that?" I look at her. "How could you tell Imrana to be a fucking hooker?"

"She's not a hooker. She's an escort." Sabrina doesn't return my look. She glimpses at herself in her rear-view mirror, tousling her hair. "And I didn't tell her nothing. Respecting her choice is all I did. She wants to live on her own and she knows that this is fast money."

"Why didn't you tell her the truth about what's gonna happen to her? She's gonna be dead in the eyes like all the other zombies here; like you were in that strip club."

Sabrina smacks her lips to show that she's not affected by what I just said. "Not all brown girls are the same, Farina. Maybe I couldn't take it, but that doesn't mean that Imrana can't. I know her better than anybody else. This is her dream job. All her life she's wanted guys to want her, and now her wish has come true. She's gonna be a star."

I angrily object, "The kind of guys she wanted to like her are not Johns and we both know that. These perverts are all old, fat, and ugly."

"Don't worry," Sabrina's eyes follow the smoke from her lips.

She seems fascinated by how silver its wispy outlines appear in the moonlight. "A few weeks in this business and she won't be able to tell the difference. All guys start to look like dollar signs anyway."

"And you're fine with her being like that?"

"If that's what it takes for her to make it on her own, then yes. Are you the only one who's allowed to dream about getting out of Peckville?" Sabrina scowls at me. "Imrana's not as weak as you think. She'll see these perverts for exactly what they are: bills and thrills. She's gonna have a lot of fun getting rich off these idiots and she's gonna walk away strong, independent, and happy. She's gonna be the winner in this game, I promise you."

"You better be right."

"And you better stop worrying about her business and start worrying more about ours," Sabrina warns me, "or else you're going back to serving sandwiches and I'm going back to taking my clothes off."

Sabrina flicks away her unfinished cigarette and starts the car. Imrana's appointment is reaching its end.

Sabrina uses the same assertive and detached voice that she always uses when discussing the Harem, saying, "I don't think you realize how good a pretty and young Indian escort is for our reputation. I've read all the review sites and everybody knows about us now. Only the best agencies in the city have all the rare girls. Imrana's put us on the map. Do you understand what that means?"

I shake my head and pretend to listen. The prosperity of this so-called business is the last thing on my mind.

"It means that we can finally expand." Sabrina flashes me an excited grin. "I've thought long and hard about it and I know exactly what changes we have to make."

"Mm-hmm."

"You've been real patient with us using your apartment so, like I promised, the first thing we're gonna do is get an office downtown. We'll register as a limo service and get some people I know to take care of the papers and taxes."

"Good idea."

"Second, we're gonna hire phone-girls and drivers. It'll make our cuts smaller for a while, but before you know it, we'll break even." Sabrina rambles on as she pulls into the hotel driveway. "A small cut of a big pie is bigger than a big cut of a small pie."

"Huh?"

"If we have a phone-girl for the morning and a phone-girl for the night, we can be open twenty-four hours. The more drivers we have available, the more girls we can hire. More girls equal more clients, more clients equal more money."

"I see," I finally give Sabrina my full attention. "But if we hire drivers and phone-girls, then what are you and me doing?"

"Nothing. And that's the goal. We'll have a lot more free time to do all the fun things in life." Sabrina feasts her eyes on the handsome valets that scuttle before us. "A business like this runs itself once it's popular enough. We'll let it be and we'll use the profits to move on to something much bigger. Much, much bigger."

"Like what?" I warily ask.

The wild ambition in Sabrina's fearless eyes freezes me with worry and fright. Instead of answering, she smiles patronizingly at my cluelessness. She keeps quiet, encouraging me to figure out the answer myself. She licks her lips in anticipation of me getting it right. While I shiver at her uninhibited display of her hunger for money, she beams with excitement at the possibility of uncovering my ambition.

Sabrina's wasting her time, because I've finally become satiated. I can't think about any creative ways to make more money than I need because I don't have any drive to be rich anymore. I just want enough to get out of Peckville, the source of my overall misery, and then I'll work for my food at some burger joint. At least then I can have a guilt-free life with Ali. I don't think I want anything more badly than that nowadays.

I shrug indifferently, "Just tell me."

Sabrina suddenly glances beyond me and I look over my shoulder to find Imrana walking towards us. Imrana looks nothing like she does in the filthy images that always appear in my mind. She's not walking funny or wincing in pain. There are no tears and mascara running down her face. Indeed, her skin's glowing and there's a bounce in her step. She holds her head up high, smiling from dimple to dimple.

"Yeah, here comes a real damaged soul," Sabrina pokes fun at me.

Imrana opens the door and throws herself into the backseat, moaning dramatically.

"How was he?" Sabrina asks.

"He was so sweet. He was a total teddy bear," Imrana gushes.

"Really?" I probe.

"Yes, he was so gentle. Plus, he gave me an extra hundred in tips!" Imrana sighs amorously and then, out of nowhere, she asks me, "Do you have any weed on you?"

"No." I turn around and look at her suspiciously.

"How about some vodka?"

"I'm trying to cut down." I give Sabrina a blameful glance and ask Imrana, "Why? You're not feeling good?"

"No, I just thought I'd make the night more fun!" Imrana giggles. "Who am I seeing next?"

"Liam. He's a regular," I tell her, dragging on my cigarette like it's the last one I'll ever have.

Sabrina stops at a red light and turns around to talk to Imrana. "You'll love him. He's filthy rich and he's a sweetheart. I told you that you'd never have to worry about our clients. We only have gentle gentlemen."

Imrana takes out a cigarette and asks me to light it. Her face glows in the moonlight as she leans over towards me. And I see her neck clearly—there's a line of bruises the size of fingertips.

So much for gentle gentlemen.

∽

Sabrina and Imrana can't seem to shut their gaping mouths as we drive down the smooth road of Liam's gated neighbourhood. These aren't houses with gardens, but rather gardens with houses. Each home is set off by ravishing expanses of the greenest grass. I'm just as shocked by the sheer size of these properties, but I'm not at all envious. I know that the people inside are not nearly as grand as their houses. If they really had it all, they wouldn't be calling up escorts in the middle of the night.

"Wow!" Imrana gasps, "it's my lucky night!"

Sabrina nods in agreement, her eyes fixed with desire on Liam's mansion.

Before I can tell Imrana to be careful and all that, she dabs her lipstick on and rushes out of the car. "See you in an hour!"

"Do you see this place?" Sabrina speaks softly with yearning. "This is where I want us to be. This is being rich. We're only halfway here."

I can't let Sabrina continue. I turn to her abruptly and blurt out, "I'm done. I can't do this anymore. Take me home."

I can't be here for another second. I'm so disgusted with myself that I simply want to go home, take a shower, and drink myself to sleep. I'll get my condo the hard way. I'll sweat full-time at some burger joint and have the bank give me a loan. I already have more than enough for a down payment. I'll be fine. I've suffered before and I'll suffer again. At least this time I have Ali. He makes everything better.

Sabrina is without words for a long moment. When she finally opens her mouth to speak, there's a look of utter disgust on her face. She shakes her head at me and snarls, "You're gonna give up your job for a guy? I thought you were stronger than that."

"This isn't just about him." I sigh as my confessions flow out of me. "I feel so guilty, Sabrina. This feels wrong. We've watched our moms get treated like shit our whole lives and now we're treating girls like shit. We're no better than our dads."

"That ain't true at all!" Sabrina replies indignantly. "Our dads own our mom's bodies. They make them do all the boring housework they should be doing too. They cover them up; beat them; decide how many pups can come out and how many cocks can go in. You and me? We liberate girls. These girls rule their own bodies and they make their own money. They don't depend on a man's dollars."

"No, but they depend on a thousand men's dollars." I speak with as much passion as Sabrina. "Don't pretend like they're walking down some different and better road. They're still feeding themselves by serving men."

"Alright, but they want to do this. Nobody's making their decision for them. You and I know better than anybody what it's like to have a gun to your head every time you have to make a choice about sex. It's always loaded with bullets saying 'religion', 'tradition', 'honour', and all that other bullshit they made up to control our pussies with."

Sabrina clutches her steering wheel in frustration. "We respect girls' abilities and rights to make their own choices about their bodies. Don't forget that this is their own choice."

"This is not a choice! This is just the shinier side of a coin they didn't flip."

Sabrina and I glare at each other, boiling with emotion. Best friends aren't supposed to disagree on such huge things.

I tell her, "There are many reasons why they decide to do this, but the primary one is always money. We both know that these girls have no money and the only legit jobs available are mind-numbing and don't pay enough to save for socks. Instead of maximizing their profits and quickly getting them out of this business, we use their desperation to make ourselves rich. We steal almost half the money they make. This isn't right."

Sabrina hears my issue and seems to evaluate it profoundly. It takes her only a few seconds to dismiss it. "Seriously—who's your boyfriend?"

I give up and finally tell her, "You know him . . . Ali Haque."

Sabrina shuts her eyes and tries to link the face to the name she clearly recognizes. When she realizes that Ali's that good Bengali boy we went to school with, her eyes expand to their fullest. "Are you on crack?"

"I really like him," I shrug.

"How did this happen? Where'd you even meet him?"

"He lives right across from me."

"I don't fucking believe this," Sabrina grabs her hair with both hands. "You're gonna leave me and Imrana behind for a Peckville mullah?"

"He's really nothing like the rest of them."

"That's what you think now," Sabrina laughs. "Before you know it, he's gonna wrap you in a burqa and lock you up at home. Let me guess, you guys haven't fucked yet?"

I shake my head sadly.

"I thought so . . . Well, I ain't gonna give you up so easy," she vows.

"I'm not leaving you," I reply, rolling my eyes. "I'm leaving this business."

"Tell me, did Ali promise to take care of your bills?"

"No."

"So how are you gonna pay the rent?"

"Just gonna work a regular job. Live a regular life." I smile serenely and, for the first time in a long time, I let my shoulders fall to complete relaxation.

Sabrina's voice is quiet as she tests me, "Are you sure about that?" Her smile shakes my confidence a little. "I think I'm pretty sure."

"Don't you at least want to know what my plans for us were?"

As always, my curiosity gets the better of me and I let her tell me all about it.

Sabrina readies herself to convince me of her new idea. She rotates her neck, cracks her knuckles, and starts, "You see, escorts can't ever make us a fortune. There'll always be a limit to how much money they can generate because of two obvious reasons. One, they're too expensive for the majority of men. Two, they're humans. Humans quit, change their minds, and, worst of all, they get tired. The only way to make *millions* of dollars from whores is to make them get both poor and rich guys off, at all hours of the day."

My guilt vanishes momentarily. I can't help but get excited by the word *millions.*

"How do we mass produce the services of whores?" Unblinkingly, Sabrina answers her own question: "Internet porn."

"You want us to shoot porn?" I begin to chuckle because the very suggestion is so ridiculous that I don't know what else to do. "You've lost your fucking mind."

"No, I haven't," Sabrina insists and continues to speak with that annoying businesswoman-like tone. "Porn is a large step above the escort industry. It's perfectly legal. It's just movie-making with naked people. The actresses are paid more for a fifteen-minute scene than—"

"That's great," I stop her. "You go ahead and become an award-winning director, alright? Just don't count me in."

"I can't do this without you, Farina."

"Why? You know how I feel about this and yet you wanna drag me in it. Why aren't you asking Imrana? Why me? You'll make double the money without me, so why don't you wanna do it alone? Why do I have to be a part of all your evil shit?"

"Because you're my family," Sabrina says matter-of-factly.

I don't want to have any sympathy for Sabrina anymore. I want to be angry. I am angry about what she's doing to Imrana. I am furious that she introduced me to a life full of lies. It's easier to be pissed at her than to be pissed at myself.

"I get so afraid, Farina. A lot of things can go wrong on this job. People are on drugs. People are desperate. One of the girls could be on a bad trip and just stab me anytime. I know you'd stop her without thinking twice about it. You're the only person who has ever cared about me."

As hard as I try, I can't ignore my love for her. I'd never be the same again if Sabrina got hurt. I give into her as usual.

"I'll be here while you set up your studio and then I'm leaving."

"Fine. Work here until you get the money you need and then you can leave the business for good."

"Really?" I'm surprised that she let me off the hook so easily. "No hard feelings?"

"I don't waste my time on feelings," Sabrina smiles.

TWELVE

Four months later . . .

I step into the spacious bright room and immediately realize that I'm home.

Glancing briefly to my right, towards the spotless kitchen with its plush barstools, I walk across the gleaming hardwood floor and stand breathless before the wall of windows looking out. There's a massive balcony here with an open door, and the view of the city is uninterrupted. As I stare in awe at the big world outside decked with glittering white snow, I realize that this is where I've always wanted to live. Here, I'll never feel tucked away, ignored and forgotten. I'll be permanently attached to the city, living not only beside it, but also above it.

"It's lovely, isn't it?" Adam, the agent, stands next to me, also admiring the view.

I don't care too much about Adam's opinions: he's just here to make a sale. He's found something "lovely" about every condo we've seen so far. The person whose opinion I really want didn't bother to be here. Ali was supposed to come with me today, but when I called him earlier he didn't pick up. I called him at least three times.

I'm sure he's at the local mosque, where all the other men in Peckville including my father spend most of their time nowadays. They go there not only to pray, but also to protect the building from beer bottles, stones, and graffiti. After what happened that day in September, the sleeping bigots awoke and decided to attack mosques. That's the worst that has come from that incident. The best is the great attention that all the poor oppressed Muslim girls are suddenly getting. Finally, we've made it into the news.

Well, we haven't exactly made it into the news—we're just being discussed in the news by all those sympathetic white women in red lipstick and pearls.

"There isn't a more calming sight to come home to after a long, hard day at work," Adam blathers on. "This building has a reputation for being a haven of peace and calm. All your neighbours are young professionals who only work and sleep. You'll never be disturbed."

I'm not happy to hear that I'll never be disturbed. The chilling thought of being alone forever frequents my mind too often these days. Ali hardly spends any time with me since his classes started and I haven't been able to make a single new friend at my new workplace. The warehouse where I work is full of fresh immigrants who I have little in common with and so I stand invisibly in the assembly line, packing CDs all day without hearing or uttering a word.

And when I return to the emptiness of my cold apartment, the only familiar voice that speaks to me is the taunting one in my head. She never lets me forget just how much I miss my friends. No matter how disgusted and angry I am about Imrana's so-called career and Sabrina's so-called business, I miss them immensely.

My goodbye to the Harem was ultimately my goodbye to Sabrina and Imrana. They don't have an inch of respect for me anymore. I had my final shift last month, and when I refused to change my mind about leaving, they turned to each other and snickered. Imrana, as drunk and high as she always is lately, promised that I'd regret walking out on the money and the parties. Sabrina, her nose high up, wished me and Ali the best of luck and told me never to worry about her. She now has a studio, several websites, and contacts to hundreds of girls desperate for cash, fame, love, or whatever—she'll be fine without me.

Adam puts me in a less depressed mood when he adds, "But if you do feel like mingling, you have a fully-equipped gym, a swimming pool, and both a sauna and a steam room downstairs."

"Are you serious?" I ask, keeping my excitement in check. I don't want to seem like just another brown loser, completely oblivious to the lifestyles of the downtown yuppies.

"Of course. This place was designed for you young people and you like to take care of your bodies!" Adam smirks at his own observation.

I smile faintly and follow him down the hall to the bedroom. As I gawk at the majestic high ceiling, it dawns on me that I have to renew myself to blend into these walls and the orderly world beyond them. I have to stand a little straighter, dress with less glitter, and I'd better stop swearing so much. I can't be my petty self if I'm to be surrounded by all this grandeur. Apparently, money buys a lot more than just a tidy nest. In a place like this, unlike run-down Peckville and all the other ugly ghettos in the Eastside, importance and dignity are not just suggested but also imposed.

I guess I'm not a little insignificant Paki girl anymore.

Adam opens the bedroom door and reveals a stunningly enormous space. My whole Peckville apartment could probably fit in here. Awestruck, I stop close to the entrance and admire the sparkling room from a distance. Just like in the living room, one wall is entirely windows, allowing for another breathtaking view of the city. The flowing curtains, the crisp bed sheets and the soft velvet carpet are all a creamy white that radiates from the sunlight. The brightness and whiteness of the room makes me feel I'm somewhere in the sky, floating among the clouds. It'll be glorious waking up every single morning so many miles above the darkness and imperfection below. Glorious and lonely.

"Wow!" Adam throws his arms up and turns a complete circle to take in the vastness of the room. "More than enough space for a single girl!"

I stare at the empty walls and nod. But I can't help a sudden longing for a familiar face and a familiar voice. I desperately find my cellphone with hopes that there's something from Ali or Sabrina or Imrana. Nobody's thinking about me. The only missed call is from that somebody whose mind I'm always on—just because I'm supposed to be. Maybe it's time to let my mom know that I'm leaving her behind once again.

↜

My fingers draw lines in the thick sheet of dust coating the old photo album. My memory of this book is as unclear as the faded decorative stickers scattered on the cover. I can recognize every single faceless sticker by its shape. These were all my favourites from when I was about seven or eight and collecting stickers was the coolest thing in the world. I must've really liked this album because I decked it with my rarest and most loved collections like the glitter teddy bears that Imrana so generously gave me. Back then, I must've really cared about all the photos inside.

"Go on." My mom pulls up a chair and joins me at her kitchen table, placing a plate of chocolate-chip cookies and a glass of milk between us. "It should be somewhere in the middle."

It's been a long time since somebody served me milk and cookies. I eagerly grab a cookie, but just before I chomp into it, I stop myself and dwell in the cozy feeling that suddenly overtakes me. She really didn't have to serve me anything, but she did it anyway. She didn't have to do it all those other thousands of times either; all those times that I couldn't bother to notice. I sure notice it now though. Favours are rare in this selfish world. I smile at my mother before taking a bite of the cookie. "Thanks."

I sip the cold milk contentedly and open the photo album and pause at the first page. All four pockets have a picture of the same tin house from different angles. In an obvious attempt to make the rusty roof and the chipped wooden windows look less depressing, somebody painted the walls a bright turquoise. The blockish house stands elevated upon an uneven brick deck and cramped between tall, leafy jackfruit trees. Jackfruit trees. This is Bangladesh.

"Who lives here?" I wonder aloud.

My mom waits a few seconds to see if I can answer my own question and then smiles. "Your grandparents live there. My father and my mother."

The sudden idea of me having grandparents somewhere out there feels odd. I've always traced my origin exclusively to my parents, and because I'm absolutely nothing like them, I've always felt like I began with myself. I've always felt like I just grew out of the earth like an accidently sown seed, nurtured by the undiscriminating sunlight and raised by the uncontrollable rain.

I turn the page and feel even stranger as smiling suntanned faces appear in front of the dilapidated house. I know these faces but I can't remember where I saw them and I can't put names to them. The old woman with the kind eyes, especially, is hauntingly familiar.

My mom places her finger next to the old woman's face, caressing the photo as her soft voice weakens into a slight whisper, "That's my mother."

I stare at her, my grandma, with a tornado of questions sweeping my thoughts. I wonder what her voice sounds like. I wonder what her touch feels like. I wonder if she's full of energy like my mom or if age has slowed her down. I wonder if she ever spends a moment alone thinking about me. I wonder if she loves me because I, for some unexplainable reason, feel something very much like love for her.

"Why have I never seen these pictures before?" I say with a sense of entitlement.

"They were sent to us just last year, did you forget? I tried to show you, but you were too busy chatting to your friends on the computer." My mom takes a deep breath and chooses not to continue down this path of conversation. She softens her tone and smiles, "Do you remember walking around the farm with her? That's all you did when we visited our village. You two were inseparable."

Suddenly, bits and pieces of a hazy memory flash before me. I see myself running playfully after a woman, my scrawny arms reaching for the flowing edge of her cotton sari. The weather is warm and the sunlight is blinding. There are so many sounds—people laughing, birds chirping, a dog barking, goats bleating, cows mooing—everything but cars and sirens. The woman turns around and I can see that it's my grandma although her warm gaze and demure smile appear distorted. Annoyed, she grimaces at me, but then swiftly picks me up, nuzzles against my neck with her nose and holds me high above her shoulders. I catch a glimpse of a wide green field and then the memory fades into nothingness.

I feel frustrated at the tease of recollection. I'm not annoyed at the fact that the episode has no beginning or continuance, but rather at the abrupt finishing of the attached emotion. It's not fair that I feel loved and significant for just a few imaginary seconds.

"Tell me more about her," I plead. "I don't remember a lot."

My mom enthusiastically begins. I soak in every word of her description, locking them safely in my memory.

"Your grandma is a very kind woman; warm to family and friends and strangers. She married young, just like I did, and spent much of her youth taking care of me and your three uncles and four aunts. She didn't go to school and never learned how to read, but she was the smartest woman you'd ever meet. She was the only one who warned me about life here" —my mom's voice breaks— "she warned me."

I ignore my mom's obvious hint that she wants to talk, or complain rather, about life in this country. I don't want to hear it. She'll just be wasting her breath if she starts telling me how hard it is. After what I've been through this year, I don't need anybody to convince me that this is a cold world. I don't need anybody to explain to me how tough it is here and how tough you have to become just to live a life above the nine-to-five slavery. At least my mom got to spend her young days being soft like young people should. Me, I spend mine with a layer of steel beneath my skin.

I point to the old man in the picture who sits beside my grandma, his arms resting proudly on his lap. He could pass for Santa Claus with his white beard, large pot belly and whatnot. I already know who he is. "What about him? What's Grandpa like?"

"Your grandpa is a very hard worker. I don't know a lot about him, but everything I do know is good. I know he borrowed money and went into debt sending me and your aunts to school. He forced us to read books. He refused to leave us uneducated; he didn't care that we were girls, and girls, especially back in those times, weren't needed for anything that would use their minds." Tears gloss my mom's eyes as she stares at her father with gratitude and admiration. "We'll return to them some other time. Please find the picture I wanted to show you."

I flip the pages until I reach the centre of the album. The pockets look stuffed: there are a lot more than just a few pictures in each one of them. All four black-and-white pictures in the top pocket are in terrible condition. There are wrinkles and cracks all over the portraits of four babies.

I ask my mom who the babies are and she describes the two on the first page as her oldest sibling's children. Just when I get excited about having two cousins, she adds that I actually have close to forty by now, counting from both hers and my dad's side. I marvel at the idea of forty cousins. Life would be so much easier growing up with an army of forty dependable friends—forty younger Sabrinas and Imranas.

I ask about the well-fed toddler on the top of the facing page, the one with a large bow in her shoulder-length hair. My mom beams with delight and tells me to look a little closer and guess who it is. I stare intently at the little girl and she stares back just as intently at me. It doesn't take me long to recognize her light eyes, but the joy behind them is completely foreign. Her happiness is so genuine that her grin consumes the width of her entire face.

Today, my smile hardly reaches both eyes. I think I've really done a good job abusing that girl.

"I was a really fat kid," I comment wryly, feeling jealous of the little Bangladeshi girl in the picture.

I nod at the picture below it and notice that my mom refuses to lock eyes with the pale boy in denim overalls. She desolately watches the lines on her palms as she slowly opens her mouth to speak, but only to choke with a sudden whimper.

I rush out of my chair and wrap my arms around her. I ask her what's wrong and pat her back, wipe her tears away forcibly with my fingers. I just want her to stop crying. I need her to stop crying.

My mom grabs a tissue and gathers herself. And she tells me, uttering every word with great effort, "That was your brother, Omar. He died before you were born. He was hardly three."

I remain completely still because I simply have no idea how to react. I should probably be grief-stricken like my mom, but I'm not. I feel more angry and betrayed than sad. My life would be completely different if I had an older sibling; a protective older brother. I wouldn't have been my parents' last hope of breeding a doctor. I would've had somebody to talk to all those long and lonely days when nobody was home. Maybe I'd never have moved out so early. Maybe I'd never have let Clint Merlon touch me.

"What happened to him?" I ask and I stroke my brother's picture in a try to feel something for him.

"What happened to him is what happens to every unfortunate soul who still resides in the rural areas, living off of their own land. They're destroyed by a government that has no interest in helping citizens who refuse to enrol in some rich, foreign man's factory." My mom shakes her head angrily and rants on in crude Bengali:

"The roads in most villages aren't at all safe to drive on. They don't care enough to install streetlights. They don't care enough to fill potholes. They don't even care to shut down narrow streets with no railings!

"Your brother was such an energetic child. As soon as he learned to run, he wouldn't stop running. I couldn't keep up with him; it was like chasing a little chicken." My mom chuckles, revelling in the ancient memory. "That day, we were staying in your father's village for Eid celebrations. It was early in the morning when I gathered with all your aunts on the porch to chat. I let some of your cousins take him to the field to play. He ran off and found the main road somehow. The main road was a narrow strip above the lake and cliffs, hardly wide enough to fit a rickshaw."

My mom's face abruptly twists into a haunting expression of agony. She buries her head into my chest. "He was run over by a bus! The driver had no place to turn. He was squashed beneath the wheels . . . "

I feel a stab in my gut; my mother's pain shoots right through me. I feel guilty for the few tears that roll down my cheeks. They should be for my poor brother, but they're for my mom.

"It was either gonna be him or fifty other people," I tell her soothingly.

She gathers herself, dries her eyes, and turns to the album. "I placed these photos in the middle to flatten them. A certain five-year-old spilled orange juice all over them." She looks at me forgivingly and takes the wad of photos out. "They are really old and we have no other copies. Be careful."

I leave one hand parked on my mom's shoulder and use the other to lay the photos out on the table. She picks up the one that she wanted me to find and passes it to me.

"No way," I snicker, looking at the young, handsome dude. "Isn't this Dad? With hair?"

She nods and takes the photo back. She holds it up before her,

her head tilted, eyes lazily open, lips turned into a smile. I know this look too well. This is how I look at Ali during those silent moments when words are nothing but interruptions.

"After what happened with Omar, your father knew what had to be done. As soon as he found out that I was pregnant with you, he filled out his immigration papers." My mom makes sure that her piercing hazel eyes meet mine. "He left his job as the head doctor of our village hospital to become nothing but a pair of hands for hire. He slaved in factories for two years, carrying heavy things all day, more a mule than a human being. Do you understand what happens to people when their dignity is ripped away from them? Just because they want a better life?"

Actually, I do. I know exactly what happens to people when their dignity is ripped away from them—all because they want a better life.

I remember the deadness in the Employees' eyes as the words flow out of me, "They become angry and frustrated. They begin to question themselves, and the entire system in which they live. Sooner or later they begin to hate. The hatred grows and grows until it eats up all other emotions. It becomes difficult to feel any- thing else . . . and if they do feel something else, they don't think they're obligated to show it to the world that so coldly abandoned them."

My mom stares at me with something that resembles pride. "Very good."

I'm a little surprised at myself. After all these years of confusion and resentment, I can explain my father's negligence in just one paragraph. More importantly, I can empathize with him. I hated everything too while I was working at Nelly's Deli. I was worried about my survival. I became hard too; so hard that I joined the Harem with an excited grin.

Should Imrana hate me for what I've done?

"Your father loves you. He gave up his status and every last bit of his spirit to save you. He refused to let you suffer the inequalities in our country. We refused to lose you like we lost your brother." My mom puts down my dad's photo and hangs her head listlessly. "We didn't realize then that there is more than one way to lose a child."

I shake my head to disagree. "You haven't lost me, Amu. Just because I'm trying to find myself doesn't mean that I'm getting rid of you."

"You're trying to 'find yourself'?" My mom scoffs. "Our children here are too eager to move forward. You don't understand that the future is just a concept; the past is the only concrete place where you can map yourself. You're all trying to move up a ladder of power, and you, Farina, with your light skin, your perfect English, willingness to drink and dress immodestly, you can comfortably stand at the top. But if you forget or ignore your past, you've kicked that ladder away and caused a big problem for yourself. You're now living a life pretending to own somebody else's life. You're lying to yourself. You will never bind with history; you will float above it like a balloon—shapeless, air-filled, and so easily destructible."

"Well, is it really my fault?" I snap back furiously. "You and Dad kicked that ladder away when you brought me here. I'm not ignoring my past—I just don't know shit about it."

"You're absolutely right, it is our fault," my mom admits to my surprise. She grabs the photo album and browses through the pictures of her village. "There's only one way to fix this. There's only one way to help you 'find yourself'."

"You're gonna send me on a vacation there?" I joke.

My mom shakes her head and tells me to sit down again. "Let's go back. Your father and I have already discussed this. You're not in university; we're sick of working like dogs—there is no reason for us to be here anymore. We're just staying here in vain."

I stare at my mom in disbelief. Just when I thought that she was becoming more understanding and selfless, she dares propose something like this. Sure, life here is hard. Sure, I have a humble job and I'll never be a doctor. Sure, I could use a few lessons about Bangladesh, but this is where I belong. And indeed I have a huge reason to be here. I'll never find another Ali.

"I came here to tell you something today," I tell her sternly as I put on my jacket. "I'm putting the down payment on a condo downtown. Just thought you had the right to know."

My mom looks at me without showing any emotion. "How can you afford a condo?"

I have no answer for her. She already knows that whatever the truth is, it isn't something that she wants to hear. She stands up and walks me to the door. She has let it go.

I wish she didn't let me off the hook this fast. All this time, her and my father's worries, suspicions, attempts to constrict me were just love in disguise. It was always just love. Dad loves me and how I wish I could tell him I forgive him.

She kisses my forehead, the same way she always did when I was a kid, and smiles at me proudly. "Just do the right thing. Wherever you are in the world, respect yourself and respect everybody else. We're all just God's imperfect creatures."

THIRTEEN

We return to the work floor from lunch. The walks back from our breaks always remind me of the end of elementary school recesses. The cool kids, in this case the large group of newly immigrated Pakistani and Indian Aunties, laugh and chat together at the back of the line. The wallflowers, the few white and black workers, stroll around the middle and complain about how the cool kids are too loud. And finally, the weird kid that nobody likes, me, drags her heels at the front.

I think I prefer factory work to service work. At least while hidden here in this warehouse, I can do my crappy job without an audience. I don't want anybody to see the joke of a task I do all day. CD and DVD covers come gliding down a conveyor belt and all I do is stick in the proper CD or DVD into its cover. The poor souls next to me close it. And the poor souls beside them put it neatly into a bin. There are fifteen stations that do the exact same thing. We're all just puny, insignificant parts of a puny, insignificant human machinery. But I guess it isn't that bad. At least I'm not getting rich at the expense of somebody's private parts. My mind's asleep, my legs are tired, but, God knows, my conscience is clear.

I'm not angry anymore, but my frustration isn't completely gone. I still haven't found my freedom. While I'm more than willing to spend eight hours in this hell for the sake of my beautiful condo, I know that I'm still locked up in the jail. I haven't reached my breaking point yet, but I know that it's coming. I can already feel the boredom and that terrifying awareness of my unimportance scratching away at my newfound peace.

We put on our gloves as the belt begins to roll. The only thing that keeps me from going insane is the music on the radio and the chatter of the women on my station. They talk about the same stuff that the Hags at the deli talked about, but for some reason I find it interesting this time around. I have a sudden interest in babies, cooking, and husbands.

The woman responsible for stacking the bins, a very talkative Auntie in her late forties, groans in her strong Indian accent, "My shoulder is hurting again."

The woman next to me asks her if she saw the doctor. They talk happily back and forth about her visit to the Eastside Health Clinic. I haven't been to that depressing place in years. I still remember Dr Hussein's unimpressive office. I remember it being ridiculously small with very dirty pastel blue walls. It had one small poster, with a diagram of all the major muscles of the human body, but it was too colourless to be decorative and too general to be educational. The door didn't even shut completely because there was a problem with the hinges. The cries of sick babies, the yawns of patients, and the angry chatter from overworked receptionists shot right into the room. Even a doctor gets disrespected in the Eastside.

The hours—long wait times is what's stopped me from getting my health checked, but these Aunties don't seem to mind at all. They have no objections to the shabby conditions either; they're just pleased that the visit's coming out of their taxes and not out of their hard-earned savings.

They seem pleased about pretty much everything. If one of them buys a new sweater—even if it's the cheapest, tackiest, most generic sweater—they'll have a conversation filled with compliments. I study them all the time because there's no other way to speed up the inching hours. None of them looks miserable. Either they're faking really well or they're sincerely content with this being all there is.

Maybe the problem all along has been my attitude. Maybe the simple life—school, job, marriage, kids, retirement—is where freedom and peace hide. But like the intricate braids these Aunties often weave from their black hair, even the simple life has its complications. Maybe those are the real challenges that I should prepare for. Maybe my ambition of being miles above all the other struggling people in Peckville is just a reflection of my refusal to face reality.

Maybe I'm just thinking too much. What do I really know? I'm just a little insignificant Paki girl.

We finish up a set of DVDs as the Auntie with the shoulder pain grabs a pump truck and pulls in with a pallet. We wait for the manager to finish the paperwork for the next batch, enjoying the few minutes before the belt starts again. The women on my station move on to the next topic of the day: their husbands not doing enough dishes. Any other day, I'd just stretch my quads and listen to their ranting, but today I find myself picking up a bin. I pick one up and put it on the skid. I see the gratitude on Auntie's face and decide to stay and stack all the bins.

My compassion has come back.

Auntie thanks me when I'm done and smiles. This is the first time she's smiled today. The manager turns on the belt and tells me to return quickly to my place in the line. I let Auntie know that helping her was no big deal. It really was no big deal. All that matters is that in a few more hours she can go home in less pain. And I can go home and be a metre away from Ali.

༺

Ali isn't home.

I don't know what I'm thinking knocking on his parents' door. I don't even know what I'm going to say if his mom opens, yet I keep knocking. My patience is wearing thin. It's been almost three days and he hasn't contacted me. He usually doesn't go more than twelve hours without at least sending me a text message.

I stand firmly outside his parents' apartment, steaming as I stare down the empty hall. It's as if it's mocking me, laughing hysterically at my loneliness. I check my phone again to see if I missed something from Ali. Of course there's nothing from him and I feel like calling him and asking him why in a not-so-nice manner. But there's no way in hell I'm going to call him. I have my pride.

I decide to call him anyway. He doesn't pick up and I'm forced to listen to his damn voicemail message. At first, the sound of his voice makes me want to kick down his door, but slowly my irritation dwindles and I rest my ear against my phone. I breathe and take in the soothing, reassuring confidence in his voice.

I decide that Ali's simply busy with exams and mosque. I'll be patient.

I step into my lonely apartment, and that voice in my head once again begins to taunt me, "You're back to square one, ain't you?"

Home feels the same as work. There's nobody here who cares about how I'm doing. Nobody could care less about my feelings. I'm just needed to take care of the never-ending chores. The garbage needs to be thrown down the chute, bills need to be paid, the thawed chicken in the kitchen sink needs to be put in the oven.

I put down my purse, take off my jacket, and fall into my couch with a loud moan as my legs finally get the rest they need. I take my jeans off and let my legs stretch out freely. For a few minutes I feel completely at peace, but then a very scary set of questions hits me: what if life doesn't change at the condo? What if the loneliness and boredom follow me wherever I go? What if my career as Dr Ali's housewife doesn't work out?

The only thing that'll put the thoughts on hold is alcohol. I haven't touched any in months for a long list of reasons. At the top of the list is the fact that I haven't had the need to numb my brain. I've been so happy about my decision to leave the Harem. I've been so happy envisioning my future with Ali. I've been so happy that my mother and I started talking again. But now I'm beginning to think that a sinner like me isn't meant to be happy.

There's an unopened bottle of gin hidden somewhere in my bedroom. I remember one of the Employees leaving it there. I'm tempted to go and grab it, chug it down, and choke my worries. I won't do it though. Not tonight. Not this time. I've got to think about that grandma, that grandpa, and those forty cousins out there. I don't think they'd be too proud about me passing out on the couch. And I'm sure that the bright-eyed girl with the bow in her hair would be completely devastated. I'm finished letting her down.

Yet I need something to fill this dreadful vacancy inside. I need to feel my heart pumping; to remind myself that I'm still young and alive. It's hard to believe that, just a little over a year ago, doing absolutely nothing but talking with Sabrina and Imrana on a sunny day made me feel like my life was on oiled wheels, gliding up that hill we all have to climb. It's even harder to believe that I regained that naivety with Ali, one boy among billions. And now I'm sitting here alone and shivering with need, wondering where all that hope went.

After resting my legs a little longer, I force myself up and return to the couch with my brand-new laptop. I search for what my body and mind crave at this moment: love-making. I type "love-making," and not sex, because it's not the action I need but the emotion. I wish so bad that Ali would touch me and reassure me of his love, my beauty, our future. These are the things I can't stand to have doubts about right now.

I'm disappointed. All that shows up are tips and guides on love-making. There are no videos or images to heal me. I give up on my search after ten or so pages of articles by self-proclaimed love experts and sneaky businessmen who are just out to sell candles. I guess there just isn't a market for erotica with love in a world where girls and boys fuck for every reason but.

I search for "sex" and I'm given exactly what I expected: girls on their knees sucking on cocks, girls happily smiling with cum in their eyes, girls getting fucked in their assholes, and so on. There are hardly any handsome male faces to help me fantasize about Ali. The only parts of men that are shown and focused on are their oversized dicks and muscular thighs.

Nobody here is meant to be viewed as a normal human being, or one of "God's imperfect creatures." The men are meaningless symbols of artificial power. What company are these guys the CEOs of? What have they really achieved in their lives? The women are only slaves to the men's pleasure. They've been bought to be controlled, used and thrown away. Do they really enjoy having a stranger's nine-inch-long penis in their rectums? Is this the "pleasure" that we're finally free to seek?

I can't help but get turned on by this drivel. This is how I let Clint Merlon treat me and I even pretended to enjoy it. These are the first images a curious eleven-year-old gets when she sneaks into her school's computer lab and researches the birds and the bees. This is sex as I know it.

FOURTEEN

I never thought I'd walk down these stone-paved streets again. I'm not overwhelmed with joy at reuniting with this old friend. University isn't really a friend anyway. No, he's just a beefy bully who maintains his status by stealing the less powerful children's self-confidence and lunch money.

It's now been well over two weeks since Ali called me and I'm here for answers. Wise-ass probably forgot that I know his entire schedule and it's not hard to find out where lectures are held. I don't even miss him anymore; I'm just downright pissed off. I haven't done anything to deserve this silent treatment. The last time we saw each other it was all hugs and kisses and now I'm being treated like I mean nothing to him. I've given up way too much to mean nothing to him.

I stomp down the campus main street, not even bothering to dodge the oncoming colony of waddling penguins. It's exam time and nobody cares who or what they walk into.

I look at all the worried brown faces in the crowd. All that's on their minds are the grades to help them get that degree—that coveted piece of paper that'll make them a lot smarter than everybody else, a lot more important, and a whole lot richer. They walk with their chins up, proud of that unbreakable ambition. But actually, that fire inside them isn't ambition, it's just greed. It's greed masked as ambition because they're walking straight for that money.

A very few walk facing everywhere but straight ahead. They didn't rush here for the gold. Their great need is to quench their burning curiosity. They are the ones who actually belong here, but they're not going to succeed because their gold is the cry of a guitar, the colours on a canvas . . . words on paper. Inspiration and beauty.

Of course the blind and brainwashed will say that passion doesn't make the world go around. They'll say that if everybody followed their passion, the world simply wouldn't run. But they'll never stop and ask who the world is running for. What is being preserved and why? What is being gained for the kids by upholding a system that isn't fair? Where's the good in oiling a machine that lets a few own the world and the rest work for them? Do any of these "realistic" penguins understand the realities of the poor?

I'm happy I left this place and I'm pleased with my decision to never return. I'd rather be poor and wear my own skin than rich and wear somebody else's shoulder pads. Extra money isn't that great. I've got an excessively huge condo waiting for me and I've got absolutely nothing to fill it with. I've got absolutely nothing.

The sun's out today and the temperature isn't that low, but the wind chill is numbing the tip of my nose. Relieved, I step into the building where I know Ali's sitting warmly in his biology class. I wait outside his classroom with my arms crossed, pacing back and forth along the corridor. If I didn't know that his exam will be done in a few seconds, I'd storm right in and let everybody know what a cold and negligent asshole he is. But I'll be nice and save him from the embarrassment—I know that all he cares about is his stupid reputation.

The nerds come out from their dungeon one by one and then in twos and then in bunches. They hold the door for each other ever so politely as if that's an essential for the orderly world they don't really seek. If you ask to borrow their books overnight or photocopy their notes, they're suddenly not so polite anymore. They just pretend like they're citizens of the world because everybody knows that that's the right thing to be. In reality, they serve nobody but themselves. I cringe at my memories of all the phoniness in this place. At least Sabrina, Imrana and I openly admitted that we were goons of the dollar.

I finally see Ali's lanky figure. He's discussing the exam enthusiastically with a pack of brown guys. Seeing him smile as if there were no worries in his life brings my anger to a peak. I brashly step in front of him and his friends and hand him something to worry about.

His whiskery face pales and his brows shoot up in surprise. "Hi?"

"Hi? Where the fuck have you been?" I bark at him furiously.

Ali tells his friends to go on without him. Clean-cut preppies in fitted jeans and peacoats who could pass for overly tanned white guys, they check me out thoroughly before they leave. They don't gaze at me with lust like those Eastside clowns, but rather with nosiness. Ali has obviously never even mentioned my name to these "friends." They don't need to know that he's dating a nobody from Peckville.

"I'm his girl in case you were wondering," I let the preps know as they walk away and then I turn to Ali, "the one he's been ignoring for two weeks."

Ali shrugs innocently to his confused friends and begs me to calm down. Instead of comforting me, he turns his sight in all directions to make sure nobody is watching us too closely.

I step in front of his face again and increase my volume instead of decreasing it. I want the whole world to know what kind of person he really is. I want to reach through his beautiful exterior and pull out the ugliness that's been hiding inside all the time. I want to puncture a few holes in his rock-solid composure. I want him to feel as heartbroken as I do and cry the truth, not just tell it. He should be screaming with me.

I speak with my hands in his face, pestering and provoking him. "You call yourself a good brown boy? Good brown boys don't keep girlfriends; and if they do they don't treat them like shit, you hear me? You're nothing but a fucking hypocrite! You dare talk to me about following your conscience and doing the right thing?"

Ali finally breaks his composure and shows me the emotion I deserve to see. His dark eyes enlarge with anger as he grabs my hand and drags me away. He stifles my complaints with an abrupt order: "Be quiet and follow me."

He lets go of my hand once we reach the deserted skywalk that leads to the biology department's rooftop greenhouse. Nobody cares about flowers during exam month and all the maintenance workers are enjoying their holidays. It's just me and Ali standing here in the blinding sunlight and scorching heat.

My anger simmers down when I recognize who I'm staring at. This is the face of the only human being I still have some hope in. No, I refuse to believe that he would ever intentionally hurt me. He is a good person. This is nothing more than just a nightmare; a cruel nightmare that the real Ali will shake me out of any second now.

"What's going on? What are you doing to me? What are you doing to us?"

Ali looks at me apologetically. He drops his bag in frustration. "My parents found out."

Gutted by guilt and surprise, I ask, "How the hell did they find out?"

I gaze at his face and as always I get ideas that I really shouldn't be having right now. But I have no control over these dirty thoughts that, after a quick minute of reflection, don't feel so dirty anymore:

These thoughts have nothing to do with me wanting to move up that ladder. They have nothing to do with me wanting to piss off my parents. They have absolutely nothing to do with me just being bored, drunk, and craving a rush. I just want him because I really, really like him.

I wonder, though, if I'd want him any less if he wasn't this easy on the eyes. Even if this godly body before me was just a shapeless bag of earthly junk, it'd still belong to the most beautiful person I know. It wouldn't shake those principles that he guards so bravely inside. It wouldn't erase the accents of his smile or shallow the depth of his thoughts. Those are the things that make me desire him so. Those are the things that will keep me desiring him long after this hard young life passes, taking the strength of his muscles and the glow of his skin with it. And mine too.

"Somebody slipped a note through my mailbox. My dad was the first to read it." Ali's face is grim. "He read it out loud to my mom and my brother and then he slapped me. He's never slapped me before."

I shoot questions at him in utter confusion, "Note? From who? What did it say?"

"It warned my parents that their oldest son was fucking the girl across their apartment; that I was going over to your place daily to get my cock sucked. Apparently, we were planning to get you pregnant and then run away together." He gives a hopeless, defeated chuckle. "My twelve-year-old brother and mom had to hear all that. Do you have any idea what it feels like to see the trust in your own mom's eyes disappear? After all the hard work I do every single day of my life just to make her happy?"

"I'm sorry." I shake my head with sympathy. "I can't believe your friends would do something like that."

"It wasn't any of my friends," Ali states with complete confidence. "Those crack-heads can't write a full sentence and none of them own a computer."

I clench my fists with rage as the truth dawns on me. "Who did it say it was from?"

"There was no name; it was just signed: 'A highly concerned fellow Muslim'."

I'd recognize that sense of sarcasm anywhere. My body begins to quake with fury, but I won't let her get to my head right now. She's already caused me two weeks of heartache. She's gotten

Ali hurt. She's destroyed his parents' trust in him. She's about to destroy us. Right now, at this critical moment, it's just about me saving my relationship. I'll deal with Sabrina later.

"How are we gonna fix this?" I hold my hands out to comfort him.

Ali doesn't take my hands. "We're not."

"What do you mean?" My lips tremble.

"This is wrong. It was wrong from the very beginning. We don't have any intention of getting married anytime soon and yet we run around behind our parents' backs holding hands and kissing. This is selfish, Farina."

"How can you say that this is wrong?" I look deep into his eyes and feel relieved to see that he is indeed lying. I can't control the words as they spill out of my mouth, "I love you."

Ali's only response is an awkward gulp.

I break the silence: "You don't love me, Ali?"

"You already know the answer to that, Farina." He picks up his bag from the floor.

"Stop making a fucking Bollywood movie!" I push him in frustration before I lock my arms around his neck and kiss him. I desperately hold on to the only thing I really want in this life—more than any clothes or shoes, more than all those bills under my mattress, even more than that monstrous condo. I force his hand over my breasts and whisper, "We can be together if we want to."

"We can, but not like this. Not this way, Farina." Ali withdraws his hand. "Not their way."

"No," I beg him. "Please."

"Especially not now," he continues as he takes a few slow steps back. "Don't you see a war coming? They pirated the whole world and now, just for the sake of survival, we're all slaves to their system. But they haven't won just yet. They can only win if we let them buy our dignity and our identity. I ain't gonna let them think that they're naturally better than us. I ain't gonna copy their selfish ways. I'm not gonna let them win."

"Don't leave me," I whisper. "I need you."

"Bye." Ali plants a kiss on my forehead.

Without a word he turns around and walks away from me. I watch my future and my last drop of hope in men just vanish down the hall.

༄

I should take a maid with me the next time I go to the liquor store. I didn't think five bottles of vodka would be this heavy. I think I'll lighten my load.

I twist open a bottle with my teeth and get chugging. The kids waiting with me for the elevator stare at me like I'm an alien. I kind of really am an alien in Peckville. The expensive clothes I wear; the lack of a brown accent in my English; and the miles I stand apart from God . . . I don't fit in here.

But it's not like I fit in in Godless downtown either. A nice dwelling won't change the fact that I work a dead-end job; the roots of my hair are black; and during summertime my skin gets dark. I'm not going to fit in no matter where I go and that's a fact. I'm an alien whose lonely spaceship crashed here on this planet and now I'm just walking around aimlessly on the humans' asphalt. I'm insignificant. Nothing. Nobody.

The Aunties make sure that none of their children stand too close to me. They press their backs against the walls of the elevator, their arms safeguarding their precious young doctors-to-be. Nobody asks me what's wrong—they just glance judgementally at the drink in my hand and avoid eye contact.

"What floor?" I ask one Auntie seeing how she hasn't pressed a button yet.

She gives me a look so dirty you'd think I was sewer stench. I'm not at all hurt by her icy glimpse. I didn't expect anything else—I already know that compassion is dead. It dies as soon as you step foot into this side of the world.

I prance down the hall with my only friends clinking loudly against each other. I stop briefly in front of Ali's door and feel something warm running down my cheeks. Tears. Tears are what I'll never lack. They are the constant. Parents age, friends betray, boys disappear, money stops mattering and all you're left with are your tears. Indeed, it's pride that's temporary and pain that's forever.

I wonder what the TV has to say. I flip through the channels, watching the colours and amusing myself with the mix of sounds. I open up another bottle and land on a news channel. There's a documentary about Muslims, not very uncommon these days. The scene before me that of a busy bazaar in some faraway country, hundreds of sunburnt men scrambling about in their sandals and shawls, not a single woman in sight. The scene cuts to an interview with a woman in a light blue burqa, her intense brown eyes peeking through a narrow slit. I feel sorry for her, imagine myself in her place. I wonder what it's like living under that heavy fabric, never feeling the warm sunrays kiss my skin. But then, I also envy her. Although she's cocooned in some material, her eyes are full of life. I can tell that she truly cares about something.

The interviewer, an old white lady with way too much blush, asks the woman if she ever dreams of going outside for a walk just by herself for no other reason but the desire to do so. The woman nods without any hesitation but then explains that her obligations to her family trump all of her own trivial wishes. I don't hear "Islam" in her answer, but this word is said with emphasis in the interviewer's next set of questions. It's mentioned again and again in the voice-over. They're matching this word with a picture of, frankly said, quite a fucked-up society.

If I remember correctly the lessons from the Islamic classes I was forced to attend as a kid, nowhere in the Quran does it say that women are to be confined to their homes like prisoners. And I sure don't remember the passage that tells women to disappear completely under uniforms. No, it's not Allah's word that's the problem—it's just petty male human beings. Men, wishing to be like God and create great things, have created this cruel world. They can't create babies so they create violence through armies, power through governments, and control through markets. Simple tools to help provide for their families are no longer enough for their complex egos. Emotional bonds with their children make them feel like sissies. Love—unconditional, passionate, once-in-a-lifetime love—is just too much effort when girls, left poor and desperate because of their greed, can be bought for the price of a toaster oven.

So how the fuck is a tiny, poor, brown female going to survive in this world? How will I ever be somebody? How will I ever leave a legacy?

Maybe it's time to give up. Maybe all these goals of independence and freedom are simply unattainable. Maybe I should go down the path Sabrina did and dance naked to pay the bills and get some attention. Maybe I should just marry the richest guy I can find and pump out babies for the sake of necessity and not love. I just don't know anymore.

I switch the TV off and turn my laptop on. I'm drunk enough to admit that I want something extreme tonight. I don't want to be in control anymore and I don't want to be aware. I want to face the evil of reality: boys don't love girls. I want to be dominated, abused, used, and thrown away. That's what nature intended. God hates us. The only thing that will get me off tonight is the hard truth.

I smile with ecstasy as the alcohol begins to work its magic. All the pain and stress disappears and I search for pleasure without inhibitions. I search for my most degrading fantasy: a gangbang. A gangbang: the precise manifestation of a little girl's relation to the big, bad men in this unfair world. She exists for no other reason but to serve. She survives on the avails of her servitude. She has no power over her own body. She has no power over her own sexuality. She gives more pleasure than she receives. And she suffers more pain than she ever inflicts.

I click on several different previews to get myself in that mood. I can obviously afford to see a complete movie, but I'm too lazy to get my credit card, type in all the information, and decide whether I want the one-dollar-one-day-pass or not.

My growing excitement comes to an abrupt stop when it hits me: one dollar. It's just one dollar for an all-access pass to as many nameless women's and faceless men's bodies as I want. It's just one hundred cents to watch girls, human beings, fall to the camera and to the money—the fleeting fame and the fleeting fortune. I can just watch, from the comfort and secrecy of my living room, as many daughters as I want trading in their natural dignity for a man-made one. I can watch, for one measly dollar, the rape of girls by not one person, or two, or three, but by everybody in this side of the world . . .

. . . This backwards, primitive world that gives you an escape from the dangers of nature in exchange for your humanity and your dignity. You slave, kiss ass, and take orders all day just to come home and obey Mr TV. He tells you exactly what things and "innovations" you need to throw your hard-earned money at. All these things and "innovations" that are ultimately here to make you greedy and lazy—a combination meant to frustrate you because accumulation obviously requires action. But you remain stuck in this machine voluntarily because the govern-men package all your humiliation and frustration into a shiny white box and sell it back to you as freedom. Liberation.

Well, I sure as fuck don't feel liberated.

I changed my mind. No, I'm not going to watch a live rape. I'll just use my imagination like everybody did before Internet porn. It's not as though the thoughts can fuck with my head—my head is already as fucked as can be. I'd rather hurt myself than roll around in the sty of capitalist swine. I'd rather hurt myself than hurt another girl ever again. I will never hurt another girl again. Naked or clothed, we're all sisters.

I hold my vodka bottle tight and close the window. Of course I have to keep clicking because these greedy assholes have a million pop-ups lined up. I click and click, closing one window after another, until I'm stopped by a certain thumbnail. I feel bad for wanting to watch this video of a gangbang, but I'm intrigued by the rare look of the "actress." I see her brown skin in the midst of all the white men's bodies and my aching curiosity gets the better of me.

The video begins to play. I see the scrawny girl from her behind as she creeps on all fours on top of a futon bed. The camera moves ever so slowly from her glistening labia to her naked ass—her naked ass that one of the five men rudely plugs with an oversized toy. Her figure is mangled and she no longer resembles anything but cuts of meat the way her swaying fake breasts are displayed through her spread legs. She crawls eagerly over to the edge of the mattress where the other four men stand around her face, stroking their cocks as they wait in line for her mouth. Before she opens her lips to the one who slaps her cheek with his penis, the camerawoman orders her to greet her fans. The girl turns around to look right at me with her soulless eyes and my vodka spills all over my lap.

That's Imrana nude on all fours, having every inch of her skin seized by ten greedy hands.

FIFTEEN

I hide under the hood of my jacket, sprawled limply in the back seat of the empty bus. My shoulder presses against the filthy window as I take in the uninteresting sights of this dead city. Everything, from the slush on the asphalt to the dirty walls of all the failed businesses, is a dull grey or black. The only pop of colour is the silver moon that seems to ride along beside me. I smile tiredly at the moon with gratitude. It's nice to have some company at two in the morning.

I get off at the most notorious intersection downtown. Sabrina's studio is five minutes away from here. I don't care that I'm weak from all the alcohol and that the most desperate souls—junkies, hobos, streetwalkers—are all collected together here. They can hold a knife to my throat and take all my stuff if they want. They can take my life for all I care. At least I'll die trying to get what I want from Sabrina: answers.

There's a group of homeless men sitting together yakking jollily on the corner by a grate, trying to keep themselves warm on this freezing night. I can't control the fact that I feel fear as I approach them and relief once I pass them.

They didn't do anything to harm me. They did call out a word or two on how good I look, but that was just because they can and also because any girl looks good when you're seeking meaningless pleasure. There's not much else to do but to seek meaningless pleasure when you can't afford an armchair for enlightenment and respect and dignity are planets away. But forget about all those luxuries—refuse to join the capitalists' world and they won't even give you clean clothes or shelter from the snow. They won't even let you eat.

No, it's not the junkies, hobos, and streetwalkers that are dangerous.

I find myself walking back to the group of men, feeling as safe as I would in my own apartment. I take out a twenty-dollar-bill from my wallet and give it to the one who looks at me with the most lust in his eyes.

"Buy yourselves some hot chocolate. It'll keep your hands warm," I say and continue down the street.

I now hear interjections of fondness and many thank-you's. Suddenly I'm not a "sexy bitch" anymore. I'm an "angel". I've overcome my fear and my greed and put my compassion to work. I've become more than my body.

I stand at the door of Sabrina's noiseless grey-brick building. There are four businesses listed here beside the buzzer. Her studio is at the top floor, above a florist, a costume shop for dogs, and a maid agency. I dial her number and have a quiet chuckle at her company's name: HAREM TALENT AND PRODUCTIONS.

Talent. As if it takes talent to get naked, get fucked, and moan like you enjoy it. I thought talent was supposed to be hard to replace. The only real talent these girls have is the strength to deal with all of this bullshit.

I'm a little shocked by the voice on the intercom. It doesn't belong to a secretary or a boyfriend, but to Sabrina herself. She answered my call at the first ring—it's like she knew I was coming.

"Let me in," I demand.

"*Come on up,*" Sabrina says as coolly as ever.

The door clicks open and I step inside with absolutely nothing on my mind. This is the first time in my life that I've experienced a moment of pure and simple clarity. I won't sweat and I won't stutter when I speak to her or anybody else anymore because I am sure of what to say. I am sure of what I think. Not only am I sure, but

I'm absolutely sure that I am sure. There is such thing as right and wrong. There is such a thing as good and bad. And even if Sabrina doesn't listen, she will at least hear about it.

I trek up the curved staircase that seems to go on forever. All the businesses on the way are closed but the dim light from the stairwell lets me see through their glass doors. I stop and stare at the dog fashion store. If you have a few extra bucks, you can dress your dog as a clown, a princess, or even a gladiator.

The third floor, where the maid agency is, is not nearly as colourful as the dog wardrobe. It's a cold, dark office that perfectly reflects the exploitative nature of its purpose. In this side of the world, dogs are more venerated than maids. I see it all so clearly now: being cute and fuzzy gets more respect than doing "women's work."

No wonder so many girls skip this third floor and move right on up to the fourth. Sabrina's studio is open and available. The glass doors are grand and their silver knobs are shiny. The pink smoke and pink lights are on. And down the clean corridor runs a novelty red carpet. Through the glass and the coloured smoke, I see a shapely figure come toward me. Sabrina is wearing a black halter dress and black tights with thigh-high boots with more details than a Corinthian column. Her black curls are no more: she straightened her hair and dyed it an intense reddish brown with sparkling copper highlights. Her pink nose stud is still in its original place, but accompanied by a ton of other shimmery gems. From her ears to her neck to her wrists, she's decked in heavy jewellery. She looks like a million bucks.

She opens the door and we stare quietly at each other. I can hear a crowd of people chatting and laughing loudly inside. I hear music play. It's an energetic techno beat—the type of mindless rave music with no lyrics that we've always made fun of. Sabrina's too hip for hip hop now.

"Looks like you're having a real party tonight."

Sabrina motions for me to come inside and states arrogantly, "Yes, like every other night."

I walk down the red carpet and she tells me to turn left and enter her office. I look to my right and catch a glimpse of her new friends. This is probably the roster of "talent" that she boasts. The few guys sitting on the couches with the girls are imposingly tall and brawny. The girls are of course more petite, but they look just as intimidating as the guys with their unnaturally flawless bodies and eyes tiger-like with kohl. They sit there with their hands around their glasses and their feet on the table before them. The table is full of bottles, aluminum foil, blades, and rolled up bills. They're all far too high to notice me standing here, shivering at the thought of Imrana ever sitting in the same room as them.

"Don't mind that." Sabrina hurries me to her office and shuts the door behind us.

The office is surprisingly simple. There's a desk, two chairs, a computer, and no other decorations but a painting of a woman's silhouette on the wall. If I didn't know what she did for a living, she could've fooled me into thinking that she was your regular professional.

"Have a seat," she tells me as she sits down behind her desk.

"I think I'd rather stand." I cross my arms tightly in order to prevent them from doing something I might regret.

"Your choice," Sabrina shrugs. "How's Ali?"

"I didn't come down here to talk about Ali, Sabrina." I take a deep breath and try to calm myself down. "And you know exactly how Ali is."

Sabrina reaches into one of her drawers and grabs a packed paper bag. One after another, she pops a fried cauliflower bud into her mouth like I'm just a movie that she's casually watching. My frustration is just entertainment to her.

"Don't be so angry, Farina. I was heartbroken that you abandoned me. I just thought I'd give you a taste of what it feels like. It doesn't feel so nice, does it? Having the only person you love just walk away because of a stupid little thing like morals? You know, I really did love you. I still kinda do."

"Do you love Imrana?" I snap at her. "I saw the fucking video. You've ruined her life. You've turned her into nothing!"

"She's always been nothing," Sabrina retorts coldly. "I made her nothing with five grand and a fan base. She got five fuckin' grand for an hour of her time and I'm gonna give her even more if she wants to do another movie. Brown girls—Muslim girls—are exciting to the perverts here who wanna peek under their veils. I'd be a dumbass not to take advantage of that. Porn is no different than drugs. If you wanna prosper in this business, you got to keep pushing new candy to these perverts. You also got to go more and more extreme—keep upping the dose. They're all just chasing that first high."

"And you're just addicted to the money . . . What about all the people who suffer from you upping the dose? What about the girls, Sabrina? What about the goddamn girls whose dignity you're crushing to pieces?"

Sabrina chews the last fried floret slowly as she crumples up the paper bag and dunks it playfully into her trashcan. She giggles at her small achievement of getting the ball inside the rim before regaining her composure. She rests her elbows on her desk and her chin on her intertwined fingers. After a long minute of deep thought, she says confidently: "Girls aren't meant to have dignity."

She frowns at me patronizingly like a know-it-all teacher frowns at a know-it-all student. "You need to take off your clothes and stand in front of a mirror. You seem to have forgotten that you have a vagina and tits. Don't fool yourself, Farina, you're a girl. You've only got two choices—two cultures. One gives you everything in exchange for your sexual power. The other gives you your sexual power in exchange for everything else. You can be a slave to the spiritual or you can be a slave to the material, but either way, men don't give a shit about your dignity. Whether it's a baby-machine, sex object, charity case, political topic, domestic servant, punching bag or throwaway labourer—they'll never view you as an intelligent human individual worthy of respect.

"Do you really think that girls are more cared about here than in that other side of the world? Porn, strip clubs, webcam shows—but it doesn't even start or end there. Take a careful look around, Farina, and you'll see how much women are actually cared about here. The only reason they're so encouraged to go out there and work is so that they can waste their money on garbage they don't really need. The only reason they're so encouraged to show off their bodies is so that they compete among themselves, feel bad about themselves and agree that their bodies are first and foremost objects of beauty and sex. And that's the ultimate goal of every intelligent businessman. They know you'll spend your money on any object of value. They know you'd give it all just to maintain it, fix it, and perfect it. A woman's skin is now literally her house. Everybody's making money off of these objects—not just me. They sell shit to them while I just straight up sell them. Don't blame me; blame yourselves for being so damn stupid."

"Don't even go there!" I bark at her. "Don't make excuses for your disgusting ways of making money. The sex industry is in a category of its own. Don't blame all of us girls for the very thing that's destroying us."

"Oh, really?" Sabrina raises her brows at me challengingly. "Every time you buy a tube of mascara to look sexy, batting your eyes—who gets paid? Every time you pay more for less fabric—who gets paid? Every time you spend your paycheque on stilettos that hurt your feet—who gets paid? Diet pills; tit implants; hair extensions; birth control; purses, purses, purses—who gets paid? You give them billions of dollars to control you and you only see about four hundred of it come back every month when you're all alone on welfare with three piglets."

I take my minute of deep thought.

"So you've got all of this figured out, eh? You know it all and still you continue to do what you're doing. Why?"

"Because I'm a total prick," Sabrina laughs. "I live and breathe the money. I never watch the sunrise or sunset; I only got power on my mind. I collect bodies—I buy and sell them. I'm disgusting and I'm filthy. I'm a man. The only way you'll get some respect in this world, being a fucking girl, is to be a man."

"You're wrong." I smile self-assuredly because I know that I've finally found the loophole. "Man or woman, girl or boy, you'll get the respect you seek if you put your compassion to work. Compassion is the answer, Sabrina."

"Compassion?" Sabrina scoffs. "Where was compassion when everybody in Peckville knew about my dad beating my mom and decided to do nothing? Where was compassion when all those guys at the strip club grabbed me without asking? Where the fuck was compassion when a pack of those animals raped me in the back alley?"

I'm taut with rage as Sabrina's words slowly make their way to me. I don't know what else to do but to cry. I don't know what else to say but God's name.

"Oh God," I whisper again and again, feeling the grip of fury stiffen every part of me.

"Yeah, that was the direct result of all you liberated little college girls and your great, big compassion." Sabrina smiles sardonically. "I don't see no burning bras or picket signs anymore. All I see are money-minded bitches who only watch out for themselves and their waistlines while laughing at all the poor girls' cheap clothes. And when we try to move up, 'cause we don't wanna be their fuckin' maids, they call us worthless 'sluts' and 'whores'. We hear it so much that we start to believe it and then rape finally happens and confirms it. Do you understand that I'll never be a normal person again? Don't you dare talk to me about compassion!"

"Tell me who raped you," I beg her. "I will kill them. I will kill them right now!"

"It's time for you to go. Go see Imrana—I know that's all you really want to do." Sabrina jumps out of her chair, unlocks the door, grabs my numb hand and rushes me to the exit.

"Call me soon," I beg her.

"No. We have to get out of each other's lives. I might destroy you and I'm afraid you might fix me. I think you know what I mean," Sabrina says with conviction although she squeezes my hand tighter.

"Yes." I don't let go of her hand either. "I hear you. You're right."

She leans and kisses me tenderly on my cheek. I turn around to leave and she shouts out a last word of advice: "Remember to only watch out for yourself and do whatever it takes to get rich. God doesn't exist, but no worries, the Devil doesn't either!"

I rush down the stairs and run outside for the fresh air that I so desperately want right now. I breathe in the crisp winter wind and feel pleased to see that it's snowing. I tilt my head back and let the cold flakes land on my hot face. I search for some kind of natural beauty in the sky, but the city lights have washed out all the stars. Everything, from this tiny heart beating inside me to that never-ending mystery up there, is just empty and black.

The homeless men seem to have taken my advice and gone to get some hot drinks. There is no movement on this noiseless street except for me and my shadow. I wander to the streetcar stop, feeling intensely lonely. A voice in my head whispers a tempting idea. Forget seeing Imrana, it says ever so mischievously. Forget seeing Imrana and go instead to that bridge over the city's most beautiful bay. Don't search and fight anymore. Don't ask and wonder anymore. Jump—the voice says—just jump into freedom.

I can't tell the voice to shut up and I can't give it a single reason why its advice is bad. There is no place for me to go. I don't know where to go. I am a girl. I am brown. I am poor. I am alone. I am all alone.

I turn away from the streetcar stop and look down the long abandoned road to the bridge. I take a few steps towards it, before I stop and breathe deeply. I continue walking down the lonely, snow-covered road as the few good memories of my short life play in my head. I see my mom and a younger me laughing uncontrollably at something funny on tv. I remember my dad giving me a slight hug on a very unforgettable Eid. I laugh as all of Sabrina's jokes come to mind. I close my eyes and walk blindly as I embrace the image of Imrana's dimples. I shed tears as I see my fingers feeling the contours of Ali's face.

When I wake up from this trance of priceless memories, I realize that the road is not empty after all. A friend is here with me tonight. I turn around and make my way to the streetcar stop because I know that Imrana needs me. I trudge through the heavy snow with a smile upon my face because I know I'll have the sweetest company the whole ride through.

I have the moon. I'll have the moon no matter where I go in this world because the moon never closes its silver eye. It'll follow me to Imrana. It'll lead me to Ali. And it will shine for me and my parents in Bangladesh.

I am free.